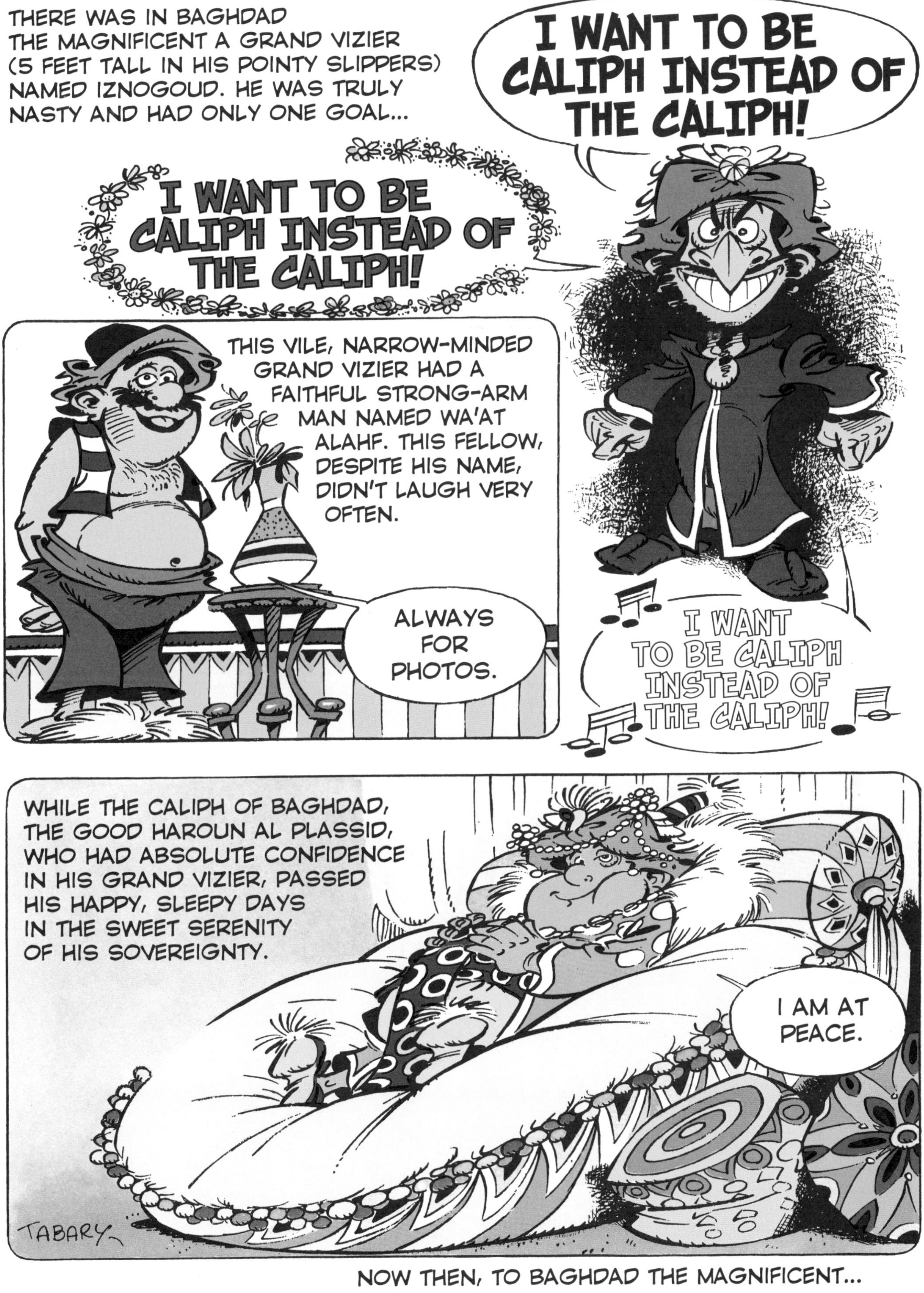
THERE WAS IN BAGHDAD THE MAGNIFICENT A GRAND VIZIER (5 FEET TALL IN HIS POINTY SLIPPERS) NAMED IZNOGOUD. HE WAS TRULY NASTY AND HAD ONLY ONE GOAL...
I WANT TO BE CALIPH INSTEAD OF THE CALIPH!
I WANT TO BE CALIPH INSTEAD OF THE CALIPH!
I WANT TO BE CALIPH INSTEAD OF THE CALIPH!
THIS VILE, NARROW-MINDED GRAND VIZIER HAD A FAITHFUL STRONG-ARM MAN NAMED WA'AT ALAHF. THIS FELLOW, DESPITE HIS NAME, DIDN'T LAUGH VERY OFTEN.
ALWAYS FOR PHOTOS.
WHILE THE CALIPH OF BAGHDAD, THE GOOD HAROUN AL PLASSID, WHO HAD ABSOLUTE CONFIDENCE IN HIS GRAND VIZIER, PASSED HIS HAPPY, SLEEPY DAYS IN THE SWEET SERENITY OF HIS SOVEREIGNTY.
I AM AT PEACE.
TABARY
NOW THEN, TO BAGHDAD THE MAGNIFICENT...

THE ADVENTURES OF THE GRAND VIZIER IZNOGOUD
BY GOSCINNY & TABARY

IZNOGOUD
THE CALIPH'S VACATION

SCRIPT: GOSCINNY   **DRAWING: TABARY**

Original title: Les Vacances du calife

Original edition: © DARGAUD EDITEUR PARIS 1968 by Goscinny & Tabary
www.dargaud.com
All rights reserved

Lettering and text layout: Imadjinn sarl
Printed in Spain by Just Colour Graphic

This edition published in Great Britain in 2008 by
CINEBOOK Ltd
56 Beech Avenue
Canterbury, Kent
CT4 7TA
www.cinebook.com

A CIP catalogue record for this book
is available from the British Library

ISBN 978-1-905460-61-8

9th CINEBOOK
The 9th Art Publisher

SUMMER VACATION OR NEVER SAY DIE

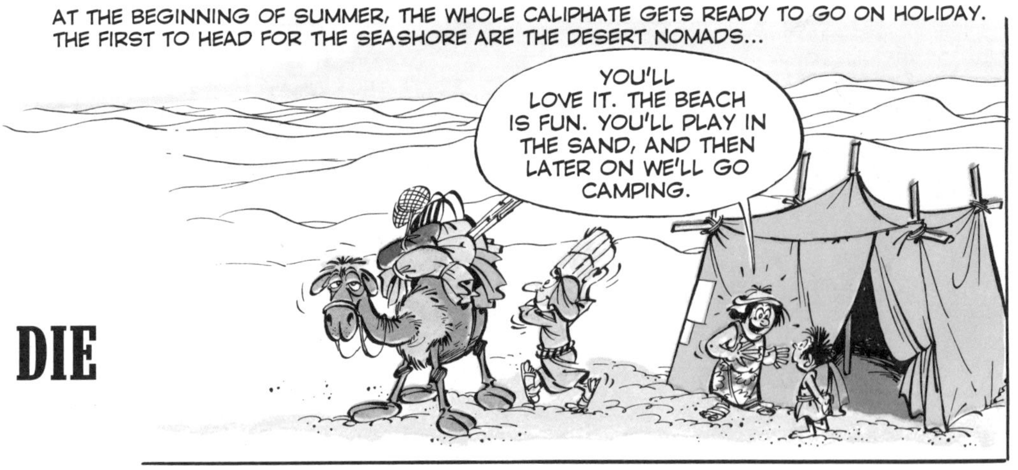

AT THE BEGINNING OF SUMMER, THE WHOLE CALIPHATE GETS READY TO GO ON HOLIDAY. THE FIRST TO HEAD FOR THE SEASHORE ARE THE DESERT NOMADS...
YOU'LL LOVE IT. THE BEACH IS FUN. YOU'LL PLAY IN THE SAND, AND THEN LATER ON WE'LL GO CAMPING.

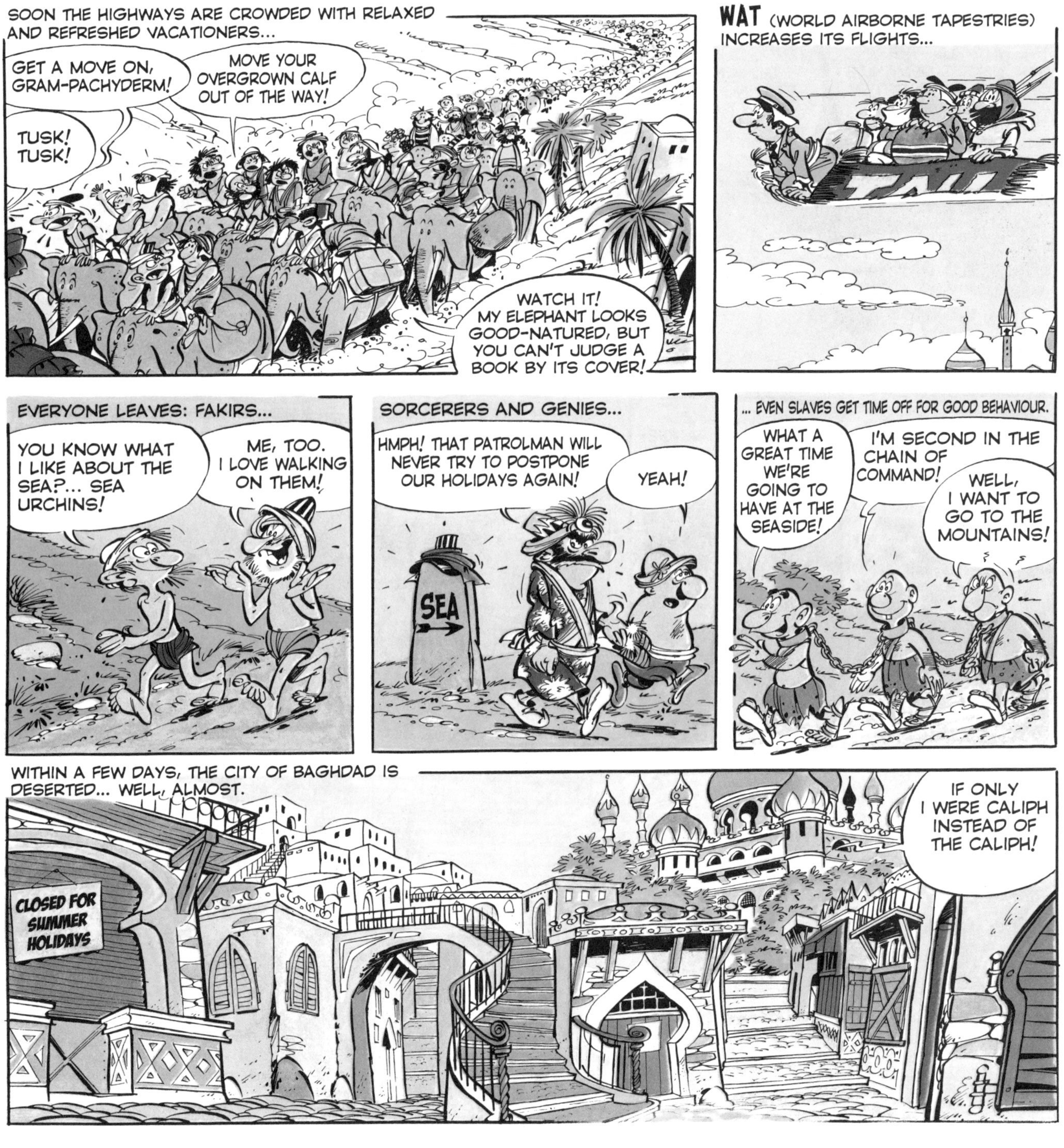

SOON THE HIGHWAYS ARE CROWDED WITH RELAXED AND REFRESHED VACATIONERS...
GET A MOVE ON, GRAM-PACHYDERM!
MOVE YOUR OVERGROWN CALF OUT OF THE WAY!
TUSK! TUSK!
WATCH IT! MY ELEPHANT LOOKS GOOD-NATURED, BUT YOU CAN'T JUDGE A BOOK BY ITS COVER!
WAT (WORLD AIRBORNE TAPESTRIES) INCREASES ITS FLIGHTS...
EVERYONE LEAVES: FAKIRS...
YOU KNOW WHAT I LIKE ABOUT THE SEA?... SEA URCHINS!
ME, TOO. I LOVE WALKING ON THEM!
SORCERERS AND GENIES...
HMPH! THAT PATROLMAN WILL NEVER TRY TO POSTPONE OUR HOLIDAYS AGAIN!
YEAH!
SEA
... EVEN SLAVES GET TIME OFF FOR GOOD BEHAVIOUR.
WHAT A GREAT TIME WE'RE GOING TO HAVE AT THE SEASIDE!
I'M SECOND IN THE CHAIN OF COMMAND!
WELL, I WANT TO GO TO THE MOUNTAINS!
WITHIN A FEW DAYS, THE CITY OF BAGHDAD IS DESERTED... WELL, ALMOST.
CLOSED FOR SUMMER HOLIDAYS
IF ONLY I WERE CALIPH INSTEAD OF THE CALIPH!

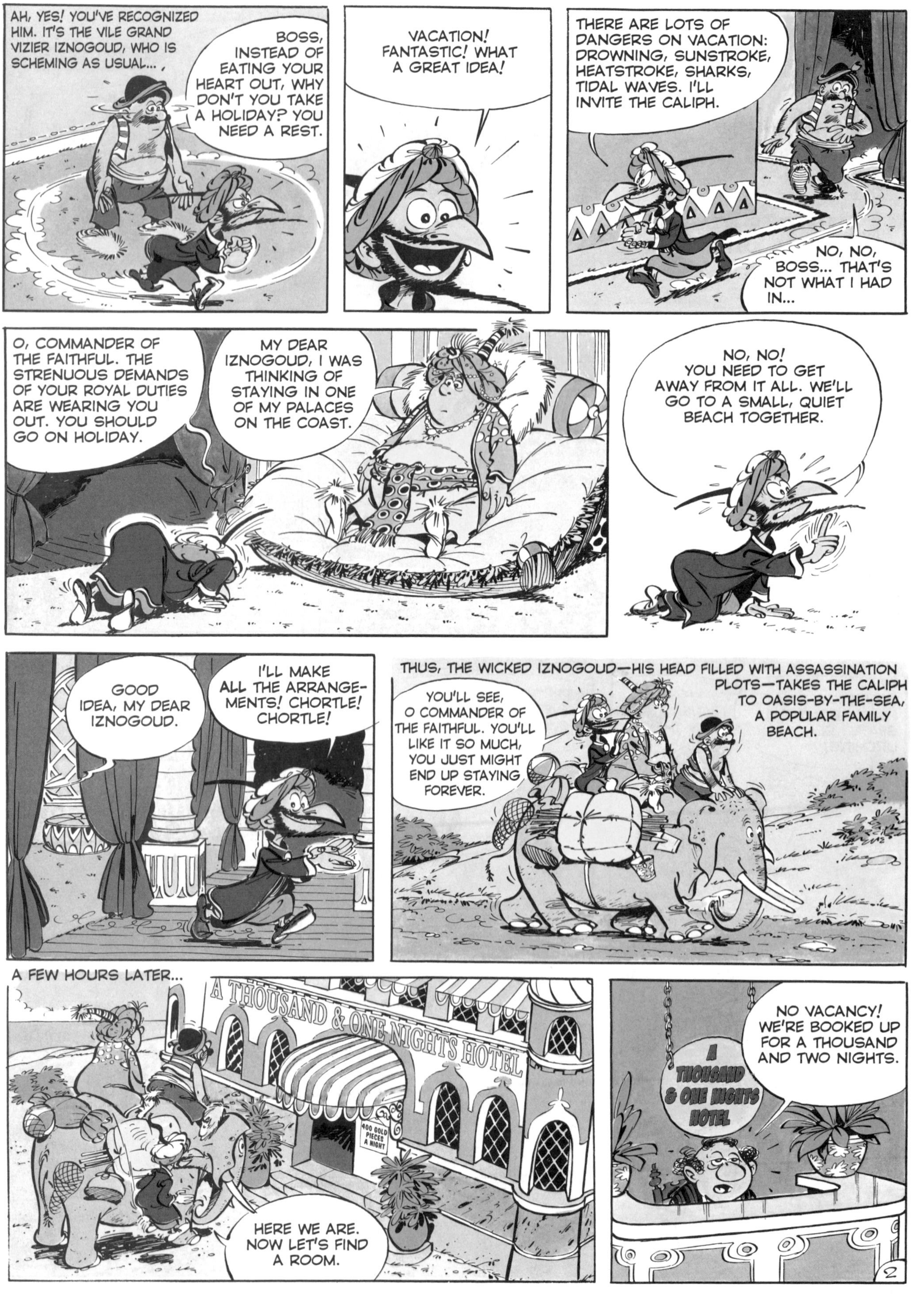
AH, YES! YOU'VE RECOGNIZED HIM. IT'S THE VILE GRAND VIZIER IZNOGOUD, WHO IS SCHEMING AS USUAL...
BOSS, INSTEAD OF EATING YOUR HEART OUT, WHY DON'T YOU TAKE A HOLIDAY? YOU NEED A REST.
VACATION! FANTASTIC! WHAT A GREAT IDEA!
THERE ARE LOTS OF DANGERS ON VACATION: DROWNING, SUNSTROKE, HEATSTROKE, SHARKS, TIDAL WAVES. I'LL INVITE THE CALIPH.
NO, NO, BOSS... THAT'S NOT WHAT I HAD IN...
O, COMMANDER OF THE FAITHFUL. THE STRENUOUS DEMANDS OF YOUR ROYAL DUTIES ARE WEARING YOU OUT. YOU SHOULD GO ON HOLIDAY.
MY DEAR IZNOGOUD, I WAS THINKING OF STAYING IN ONE OF MY PALACES ON THE COAST.
NO, NO! YOU NEED TO GET AWAY FROM IT ALL. WE'LL GO TO A SMALL, QUIET BEACH TOGETHER.
GOOD IDEA, MY DEAR IZNOGOUD.
I'LL MAKE ALL THE ARRANGEMENTS! CHORTLE! CHORTLE!
THUS, THE WICKED IZNOGOUD—HIS HEAD FILLED WITH ASSASSINATION PLOTS—TAKES THE CALIPH TO OASIS-BY-THE-SEA, A POPULAR FAMILY BEACH.
YOU'LL SEE, O COMMANDER OF THE FAITHFUL. YOU'LL LIKE IT SO MUCH, YOU JUST MIGHT END UP STAYING FOREVER.
A FEW HOURS LATER...
A THOUSAND & ONE NIGHTS HOTEL
400 GOLD PIECES A NIGHT
HERE WE ARE. NOW LET'S FIND A ROOM.
A THOUSAND & ONE NIGHTS HOTEL
NO VACANCY! WE'RE BOOKED UP FOR A THOUSAND AND TWO NIGHTS.
2

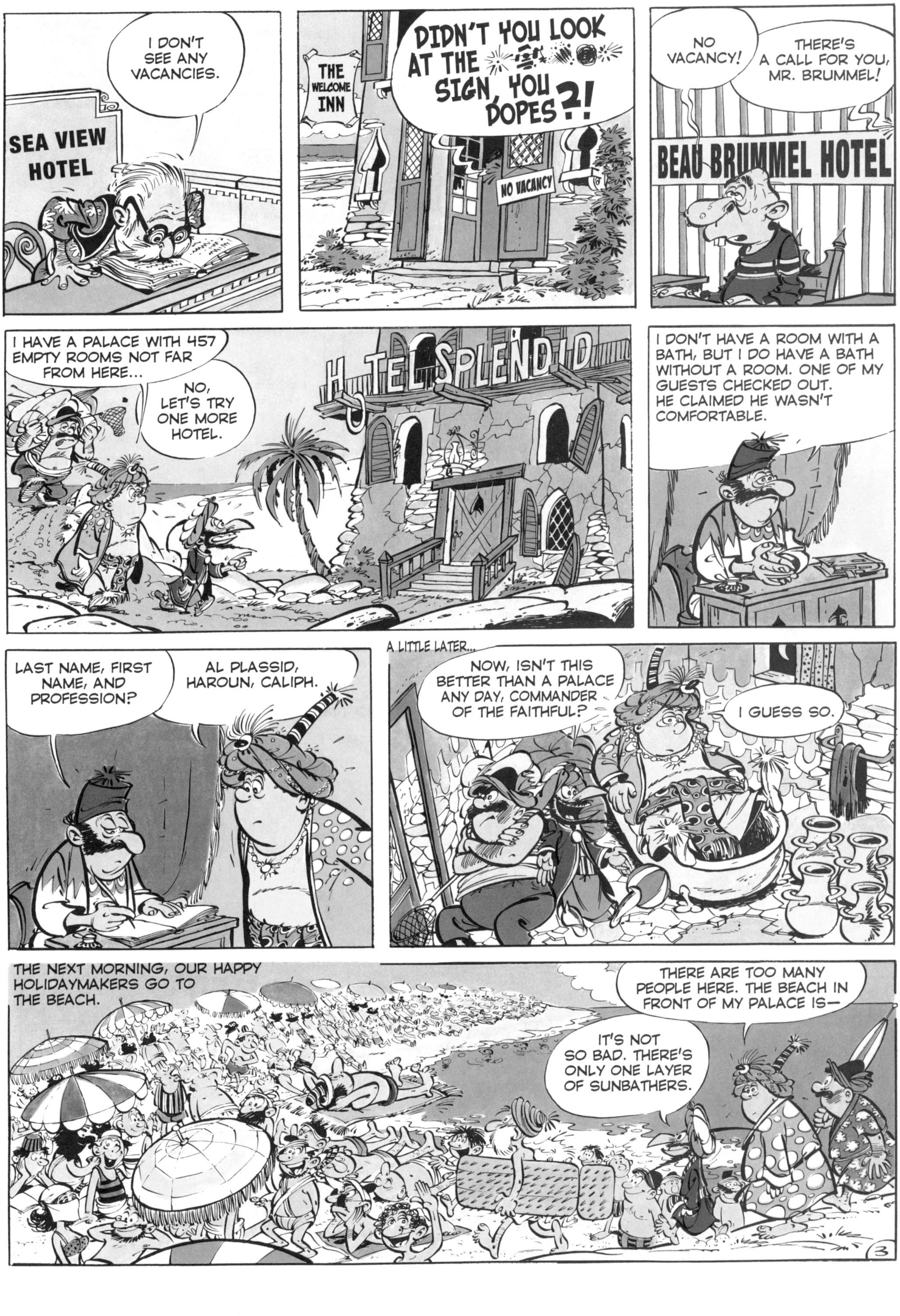
I DON'T SEE ANY VACANCIES.
SEA VIEW HOTEL
THE WELCOME INN
DIDN'T YOU LOOK AT THE SIGN, YOU DOPES?!
NO VACANCY
NO VACANCY!
THERE'S A CALL FOR YOU, MR. BRUMMEL!
BEAU BRUMMEL HOTEL
I HAVE A PALACE WITH 457 EMPTY ROOMS NOT FAR FROM HERE...
NO, LET'S TRY ONE MORE HOTEL.
H TEL SPLENDID
I DON'T HAVE A ROOM WITH A BATH, BUT I DO HAVE A BATH WITHOUT A ROOM. ONE OF MY GUESTS CHECKED OUT. HE CLAIMED HE WASN'T COMFORTABLE.
LAST NAME, FIRST NAME, AND PROFESSION?
AL PLASSID, HAROUN, CALIPH.
A LITTLE LATER...
NOW, ISN'T THIS BETTER THAN A PALACE ANY DAY, COMMANDER OF THE FAITHFUL?
I GUESS SO.
THE NEXT MORNING, OUR HAPPY HOLIDAYMAKERS GO TO THE BEACH.
THERE ARE TOO MANY PEOPLE HERE. THE BEACH IN FRONT OF MY PALACE IS—
IT'S NOT SO BAD. THERE'S ONLY ONE LAYER OF SUNBATHERS.
3

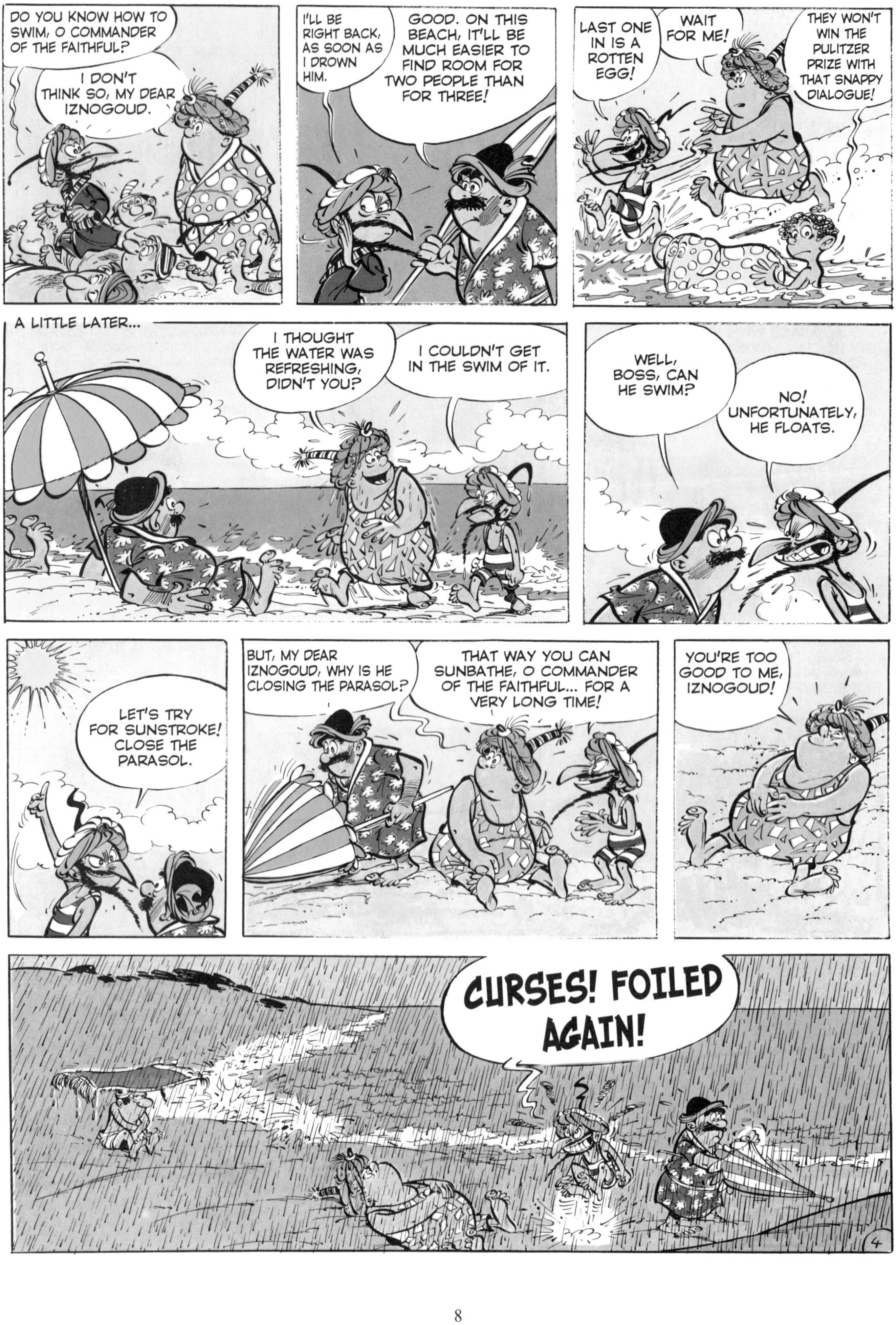
DO YOU KNOW HOW TO SWIM, O COMMANDER OF THE FAITHFUL?
I DON'T THINK SO, MY DEAR IZNOGOUD.
I'LL BE RIGHT BACK, AS SOON AS I DROWN HIM.
GOOD. ON THIS BEACH, IT'LL BE MUCH EASIER TO FIND ROOM FOR TWO PEOPLE THAN FOR THREE!
LAST ONE IN IS A ROTTEN EGG!
WAIT FOR ME!
THEY WON'T WIN THE PULITZER PRIZE WITH THAT SNAPPY DIALOGUE!
A LITTLE LATER...
I THOUGHT THE WATER WAS REFRESHING, DIDN'T YOU?
I COULDN'T GET IN THE SWIM OF IT.
WELL, BOSS, CAN HE SWIM?
NO! UNFORTUNATELY, HE FLOATS.
LET'S TRY FOR SUNSTROKE! CLOSE THE PARASOL.
BUT, MY DEAR IZNOGOUD, WHY IS HE CLOSING THE PARASOL?
THAT WAY YOU CAN SUNBATHE, O COMMANDER OF THE FAITHFUL... FOR A VERY LONG TIME!
YOU'RE TOO GOOD TO ME, IZNOGOUD!
CURSES! FOILED AGAIN!
4

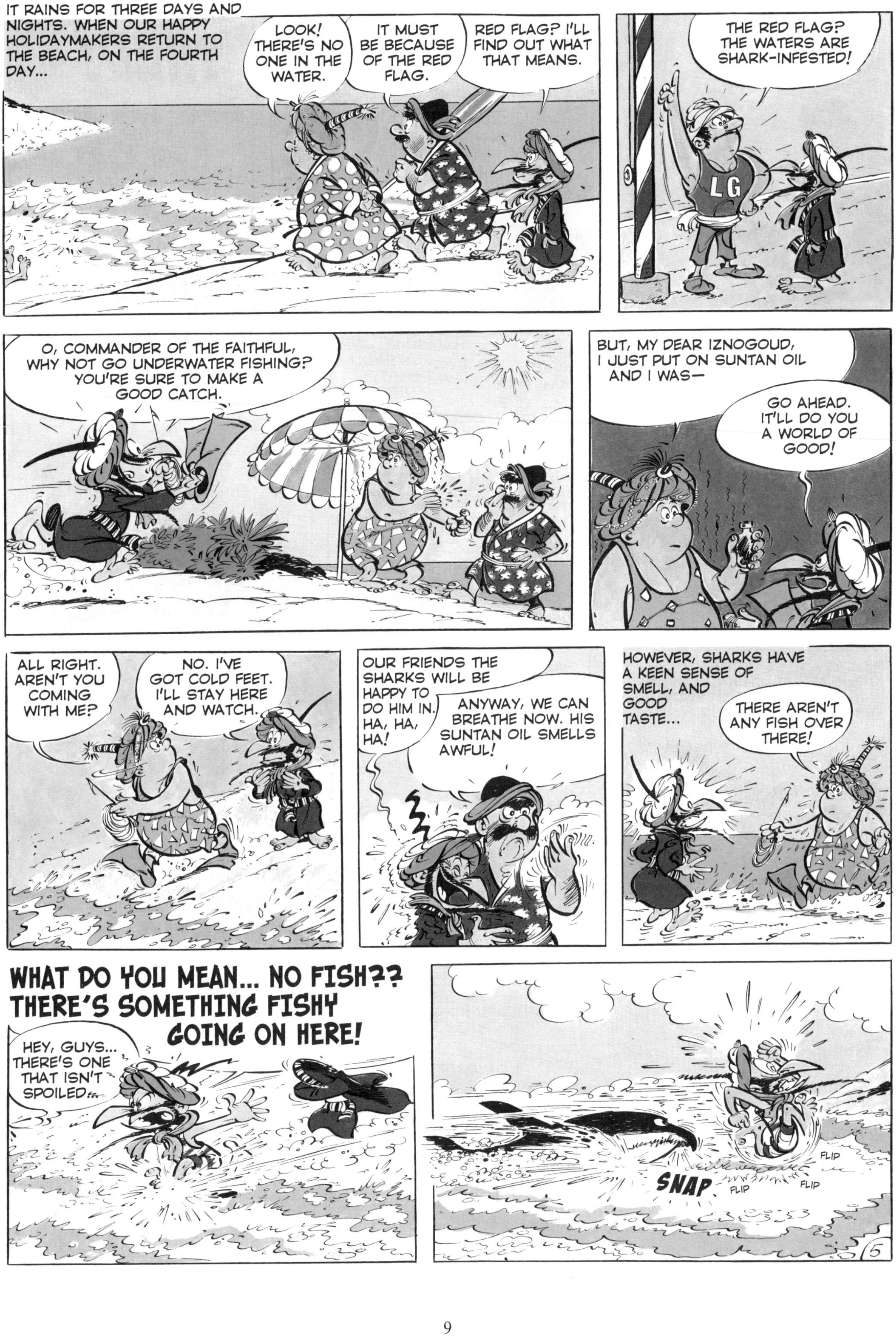
IT RAINS FOR THREE DAYS AND NIGHTS. WHEN OUR HAPPY HOLIDAYMAKERS RETURN TO THE BEACH, ON THE FOURTH DAY...
LOOK! THERE'S NO ONE IN THE WATER.
IT MUST BE BECAUSE OF THE RED FLAG.
RED FLAG? I'LL FIND OUT WHAT THAT MEANS.
THE RED FLAG? THE WATERS ARE SHARK-INFESTED!
LG
O, COMMANDER OF THE FAITHFUL, WHY NOT GO UNDERWATER FISHING? YOU'RE SURE TO MAKE A GOOD CATCH.
BUT, MY DEAR IZNOGOUD, I JUST PUT ON SUNTAN OIL AND I WAS—
GO AHEAD. IT'LL DO YOU A WORLD OF GOOD!
ALL RIGHT. AREN'T YOU COMING WITH ME?
NO. I'VE GOT COLD FEET. I'LL STAY HERE AND WATCH.
OUR FRIENDS THE SHARKS WILL BE HAPPY TO DO HIM IN. HA, HA, HA!
ANYWAY, WE CAN BREATHE NOW. HIS SUNTAN OIL SMELLS AWFUL!
HOWEVER, SHARKS HAVE A KEEN SENSE OF SMELL, AND GOOD TASTE...
THERE AREN'T ANY FISH OVER THERE!
WHAT DO YOU MEAN... NO FISH?? THERE'S SOMETHING FISHY GOING ON HERE!
HEY, GUYS... THERE'S ONE THAT ISN'T SPOILED...
SNAP
FLIP
FLIP
FLIP
5

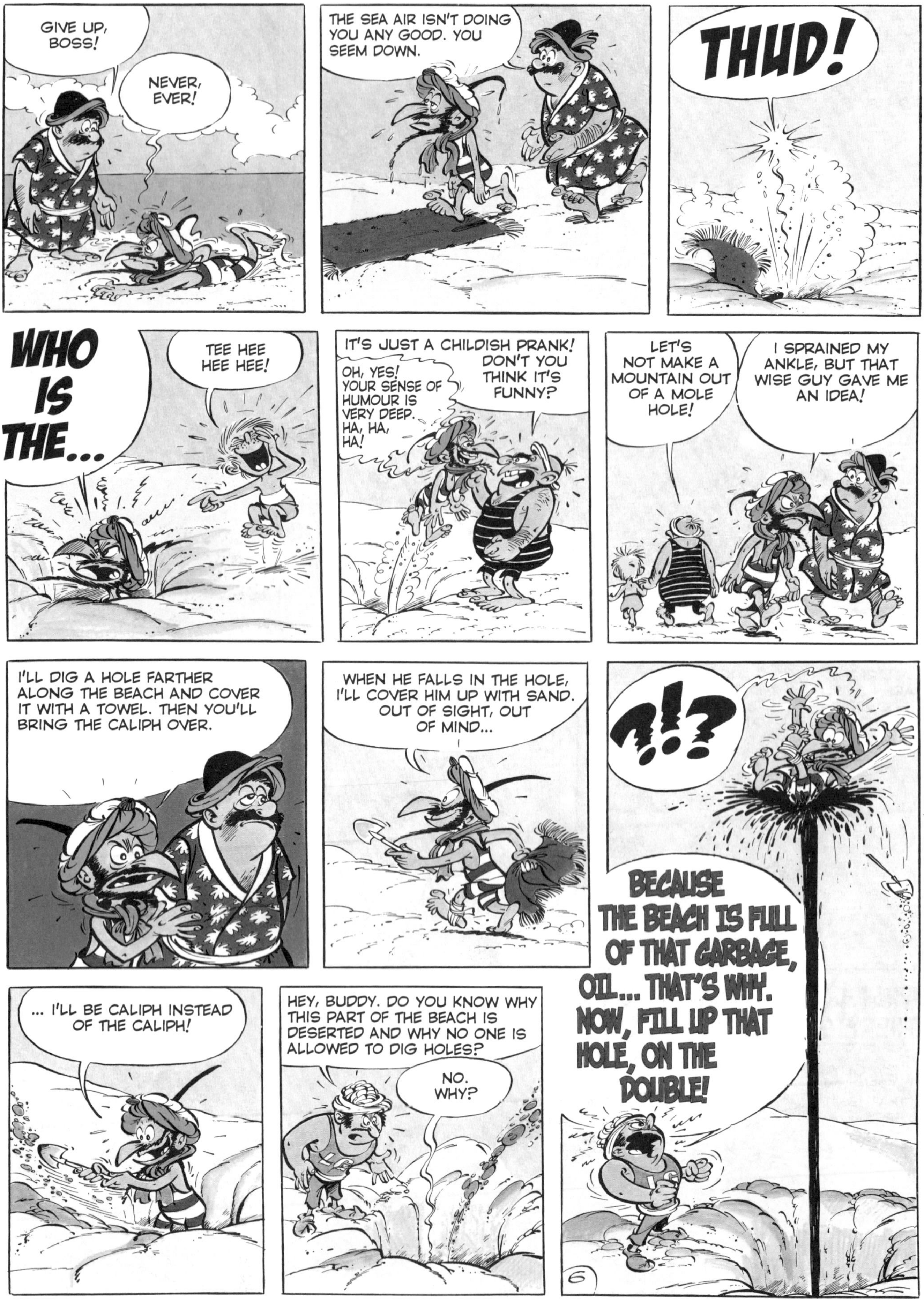
GIVE UP, BOSS!
NEVER, EVER!
THE SEA AIR ISN'T DOING YOU ANY GOOD. YOU SEEM DOWN.
THUD!
WHO IS THE...
TEE HEE HEE HEE!
IT'S JUST A CHILDISH PRANK! DON'T YOU THINK IT'S FUNNY?
OH, YES! YOUR SENSE OF HUMOUR IS VERY DEEP. HA, HA, HA!
LET'S NOT MAKE A MOUNTAIN OUT OF A MOLE HOLE!
I SPRAINED MY ANKLE, BUT THAT WISE GUY GAVE ME AN IDEA!
I'LL DIG A HOLE FARTHER ALONG THE BEACH AND COVER IT WITH A TOWEL. THEN YOU'LL BRING THE CALIPH OVER.
WHEN HE FALLS IN THE HOLE, I'LL COVER HIM UP WITH SAND. OUT OF SIGHT, OUT OF MIND...
?!?
... I'LL BE CALIPH INSTEAD OF THE CALIPH!
HEY, BUDDY. DO YOU KNOW WHY THIS PART OF THE BEACH IS DESERTED AND WHY NO ONE IS ALLOWED TO DIG HOLES?
NO. WHY?
BECAUSE THE BEACH IS FULL OF THAT GARBAGE, OIL... THAT'S WHY. NOW, FILL UP THAT HOLE, ON THE DOUBLE!
6

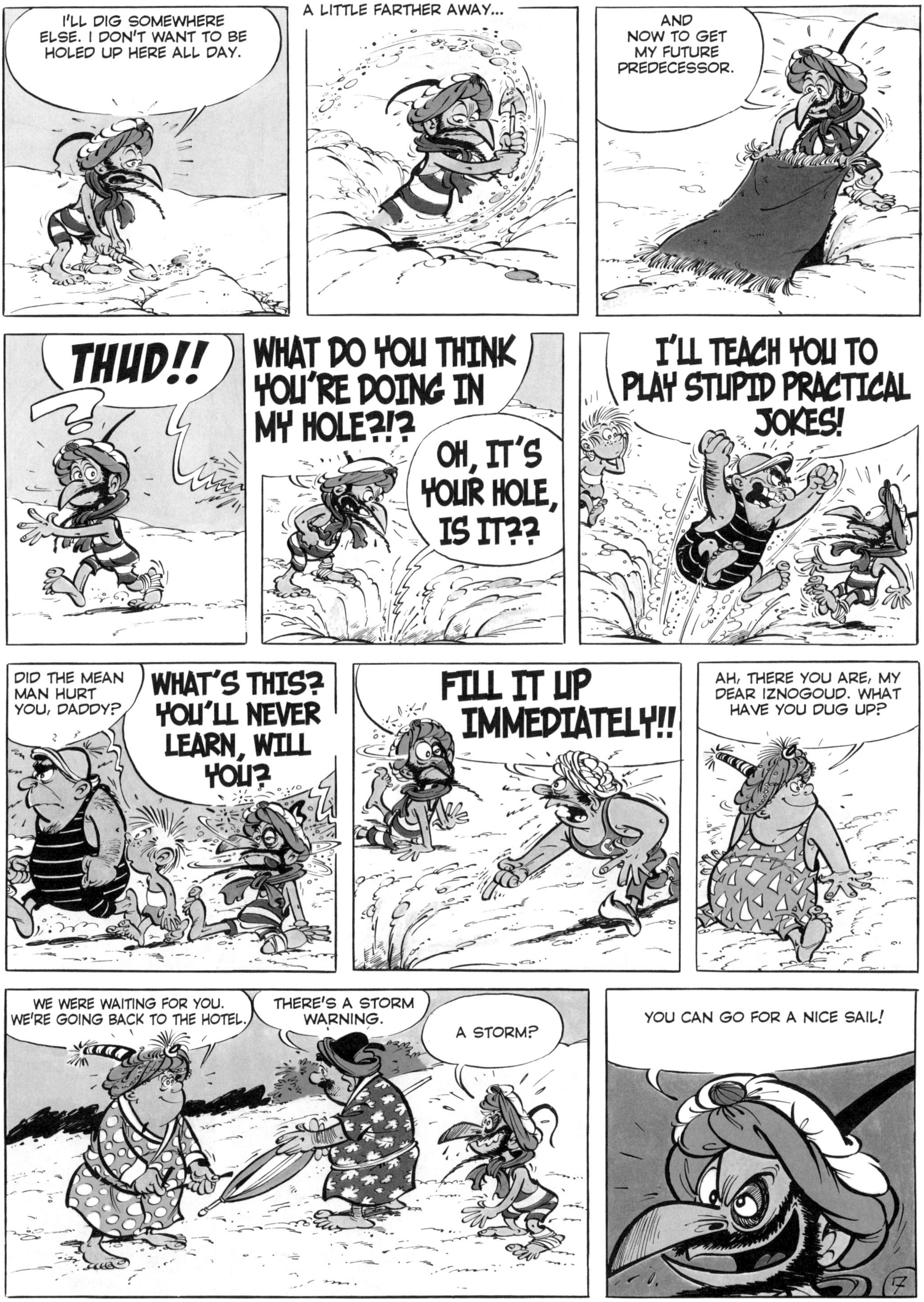
I'LL DIG SOMEWHERE ELSE. I DON'T WANT TO BE HOLED UP HERE ALL DAY.
A LITTLE FARTHER AWAY...
AND NOW TO GET MY FUTURE PREDECESSOR.
THUD!!
WHAT DO YOU THINK YOU'RE DOING IN MY HOLE?!?
OH, IT'S YOUR HOLE, IS IT??
I'LL TEACH YOU TO PLAY STUPID PRACTICAL JOKES!
DID THE MEAN MAN HURT YOU, DADDY?
WHAT'S THIS? YOU'LL NEVER LEARN, WILL YOU?
FILL IT UP IMMEDIATELY!!
AH, THERE YOU ARE, MY DEAR IZNOGOUD. WHAT HAVE YOU DUG UP?
WE WERE WAITING FOR YOU. WE'RE GOING BACK TO THE HOTEL.
THERE'S A STORM WARNING.
A STORM?
YOU CAN GO FOR A NICE SAIL!

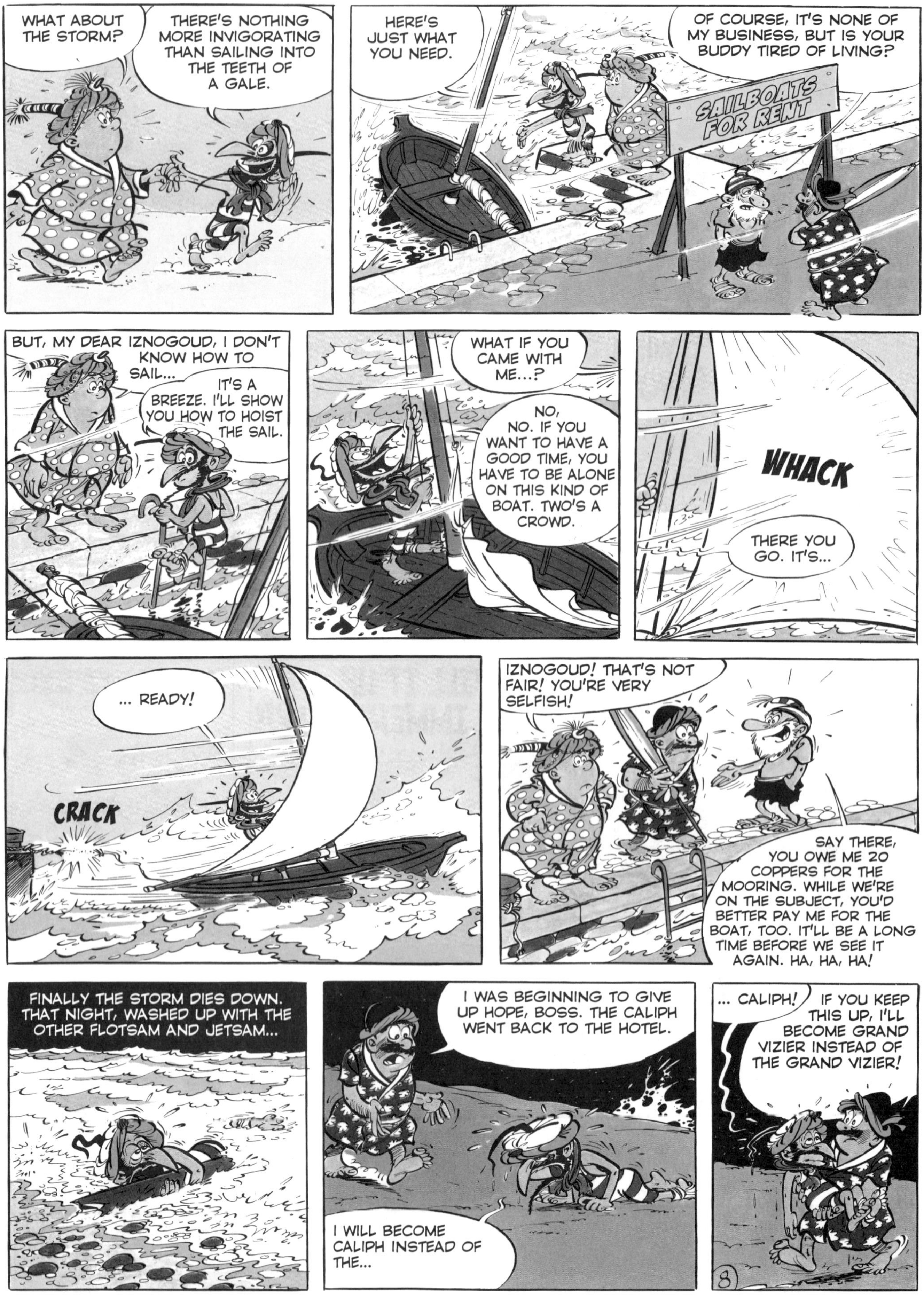
WHAT ABOUT THE STORM?
THERE'S NOTHING MORE INVIGORATING THAN SAILING INTO THE TEETH OF A GALE.
HERE'S JUST WHAT YOU NEED.
OF COURSE, IT'S NONE OF MY BUSINESS, BUT IS YOUR BUDDY TIRED OF LIVING?
SAILBOATS FOR RENT
BUT, MY DEAR IZNOGOUD, I DON'T KNOW HOW TO SAIL...
IT'S A BREEZE. I'LL SHOW YOU HOW TO HOIST THE SAIL.
WHAT IF YOU CAME WITH ME...?
NO, NO. IF YOU WANT TO HAVE A GOOD TIME, YOU HAVE TO BE ALONE ON THIS KIND OF BOAT. TWO'S A CROWD.
WHACK
THERE YOU GO. IT'S...
... READY!
CRACK
IZNOGOUD! THAT'S NOT FAIR! YOU'RE VERY SELFISH!
SAY THERE, YOU OWE ME 20 COPPERS FOR THE MOORING. WHILE WE'RE ON THE SUBJECT, YOU'D BETTER PAY ME FOR THE BOAT, TOO. IT'LL BE A LONG TIME BEFORE WE SEE IT AGAIN. HA, HA, HA!
FINALLY THE STORM DIES DOWN. THAT NIGHT, WASHED UP WITH THE OTHER FLOTSAM AND JETSAM...
I WAS BEGINNING TO GIVE UP HOPE, BOSS. THE CALIPH WENT BACK TO THE HOTEL.
I WILL BECOME CALIPH INSTEAD OF THE...
... CALIPH!
IF YOU KEEP THIS UP, I'LL BECOME GRAND VIZIER INSTEAD OF THE GRAND VIZIER!
8

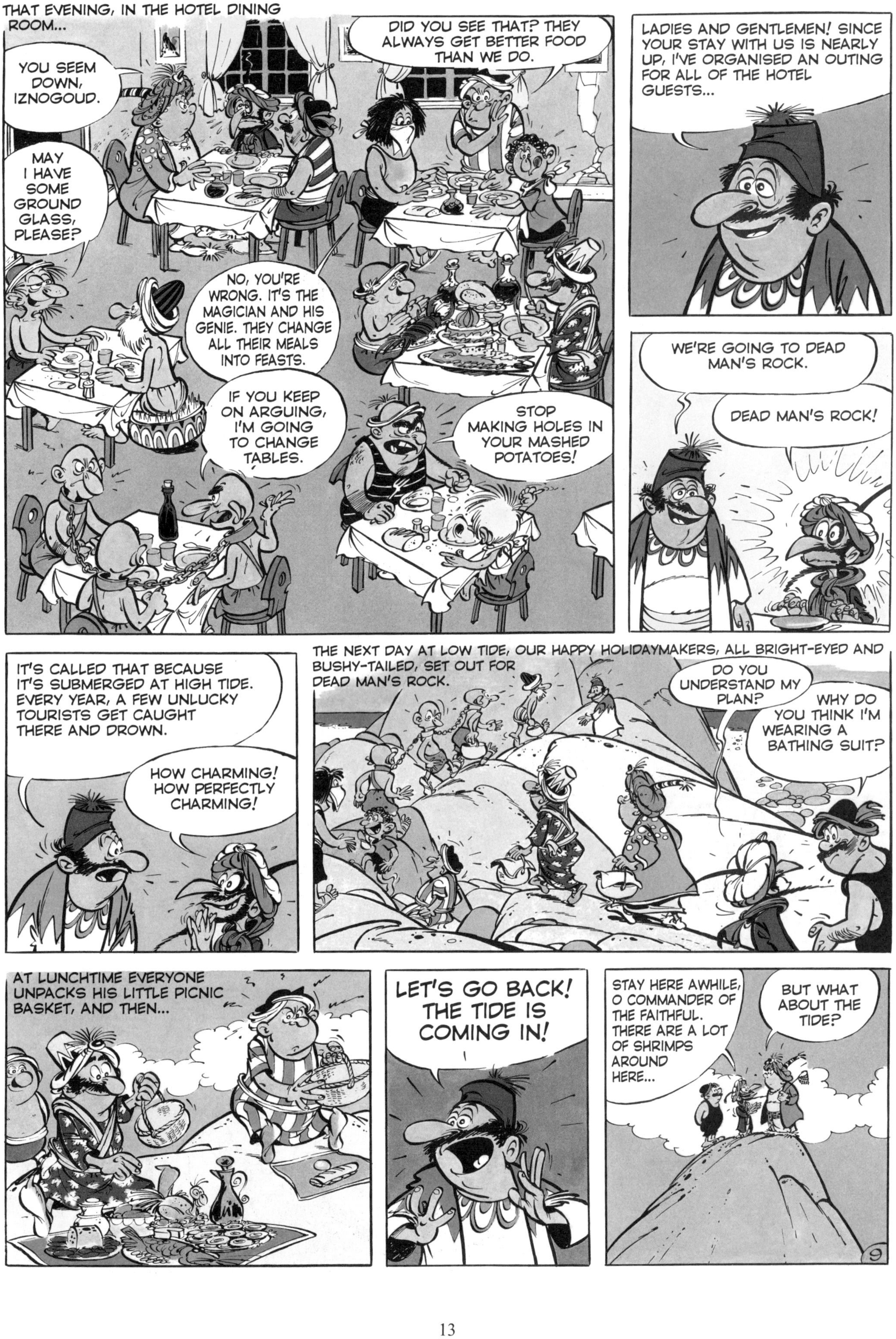
THAT EVENING, IN THE HOTEL DINING ROOM...
YOU SEEM DOWN, IZNOGOUD.
DID YOU SEE THAT? THEY ALWAYS GET BETTER FOOD THAN WE DO.
MAY I HAVE SOME GROUND GLASS, PLEASE?
NO, YOU'RE WRONG. IT'S THE MAGICIAN AND HIS GENIE. THEY CHANGE ALL THEIR MEALS INTO FEASTS.
IF YOU KEEP ON ARGUING, I'M GOING TO CHANGE TABLES.
STOP MAKING HOLES IN YOUR MASHED POTATOES!
LADIES AND GENTLEMEN! SINCE YOUR STAY WITH US IS NEARLY UP, I'VE ORGANISED AN OUTING FOR ALL OF THE HOTEL GUESTS...
WE'RE GOING TO DEAD MAN'S ROCK.
DEAD MAN'S ROCK!
IT'S CALLED THAT BECAUSE IT'S SUBMERGED AT HIGH TIDE. EVERY YEAR, A FEW UNLUCKY TOURISTS GET CAUGHT THERE AND DROWN.
HOW CHARMING! HOW PERFECTLY CHARMING!
THE NEXT DAY AT LOW TIDE, OUR HAPPY HOLIDAYMAKERS, ALL BRIGHT-EYED AND BUSHY-TAILED, SET OUT FOR DEAD MAN'S ROCK.
DO YOU UNDERSTAND MY PLAN?
WHY DO YOU THINK I'M WEARING A BATHING SUIT?
AT LUNCHTIME EVERYONE UNPACKS HIS LITTLE PICNIC BASKET, AND THEN...
LET'S GO BACK! THE TIDE IS COMING IN!
STAY HERE AWHILE, O COMMANDER OF THE FAITHFUL. THERE ARE A LOT OF SHRIMPS AROUND HERE...
BUT WHAT ABOUT THE TIDE?
9

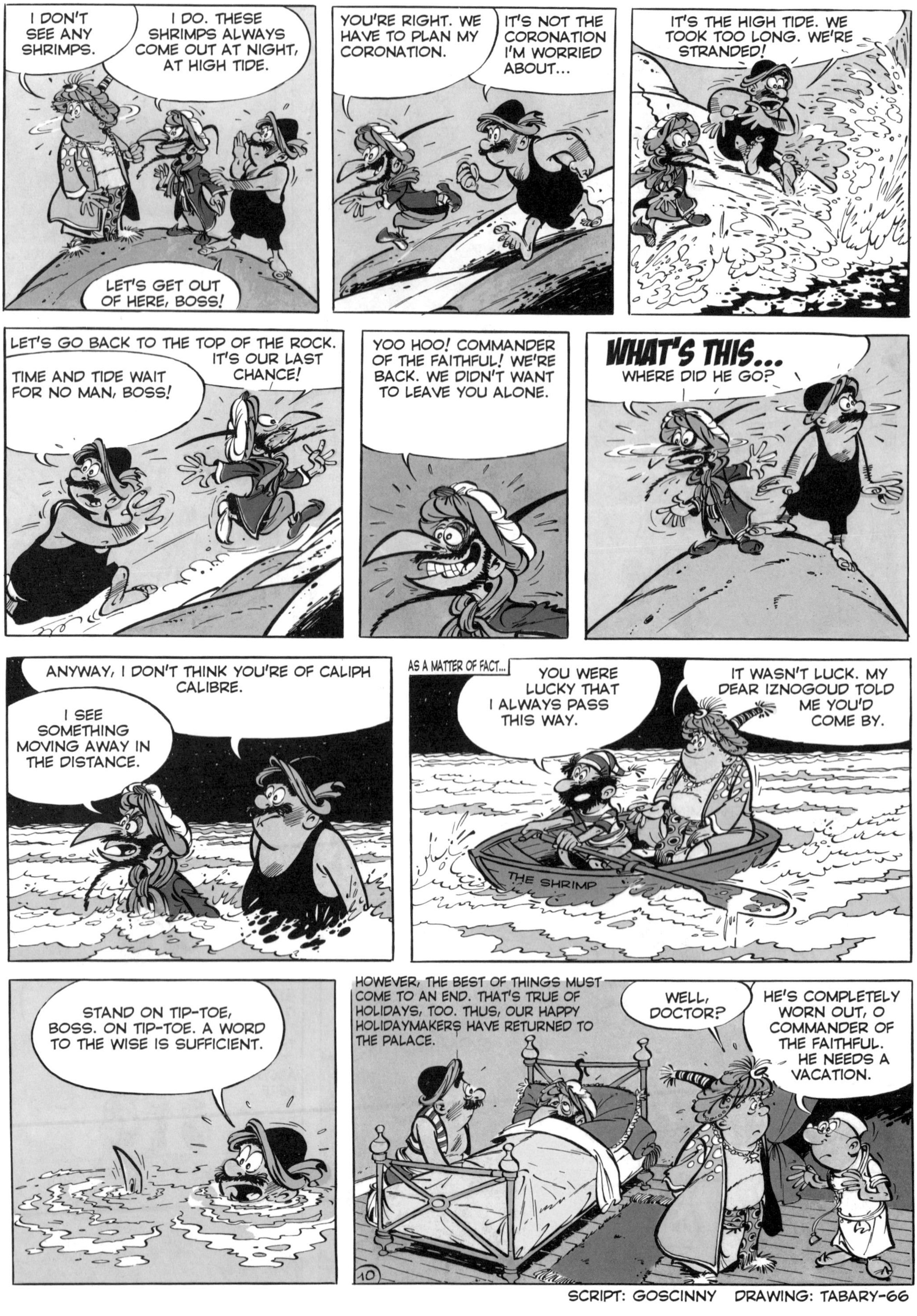
I DON'T SEE ANY SHRIMPS.
I DO. THESE SHRIMPS ALWAYS COME OUT AT NIGHT, AT HIGH TIDE.
LET'S GET OUT OF HERE, BOSS!
YOU'RE RIGHT. WE HAVE TO PLAN MY CORONATION.
IT'S NOT THE CORONATION I'M WORRIED ABOUT...
IT'S THE HIGH TIDE. WE TOOK TOO LONG. WE'RE STRANDED!
LET'S GO BACK TO THE TOP OF THE ROCK.
IT'S OUR LAST CHANCE!
TIME AND TIDE WAIT FOR NO MAN, BOSS!
YOO HOO! COMMANDER OF THE FAITHFUL! WE'RE BACK. WE DIDN'T WANT TO LEAVE YOU ALONE.
WHAT'S THIS...
WHERE DID HE GO?
ANYWAY, I DON'T THINK YOU'RE OF CALIPH CALIBRE.
I SEE SOMETHING MOVING AWAY IN THE DISTANCE.
AS A MATTER OF FACT...
YOU WERE LUCKY THAT I ALWAYS PASS THIS WAY.
IT WASN'T LUCK. MY DEAR IZNOGOUD TOLD ME YOU'D COME BY.
THE SHRIMP
STAND ON TIP-TOE, BOSS. ON TIP-TOE. A WORD TO THE WISE IS SUFFICIENT.
HOWEVER, THE BEST OF THINGS MUST COME TO AN END. THAT'S TRUE OF HOLIDAYS, TOO. THUS, OUR HAPPY HOLIDAYMAKERS HAVE RETURNED TO THE PALACE.
WELL, DOCTOR?
HE'S COMPLETELY WORN OUT, O COMMANDER OF THE FAITHFUL. HE NEEDS A VACATION.
10
SCRIPT: GOSCINNY DRAWING: TABARY-66

GOOD SPORTS IN THE CALIPHATE

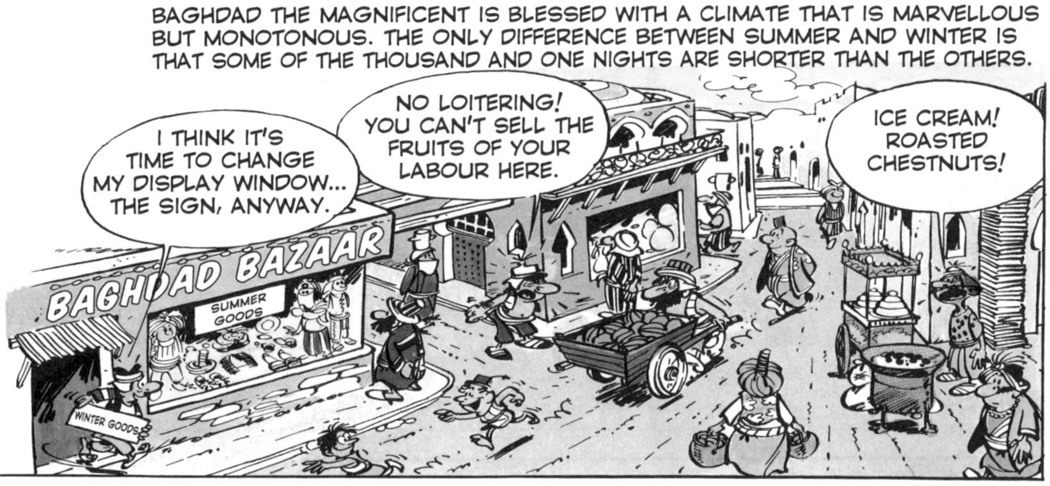

BAGHDAD THE MAGNIFICENT IS BLESSED WITH A CLIMATE THAT IS MARVELLOUS BUT MONOTONOUS. THE ONLY DIFFERENCE BETWEEN SUMMER AND WINTER IS THAT SOME OF THE THOUSAND AND ONE NIGHTS ARE SHORTER THAN THE OTHERS.
I THINK IT'S TIME TO CHANGE MY DISPLAY WINDOW... THE SIGN, ANYWAY.
NO LOITERING! YOU CAN'T SELL THE FRUITS OF YOUR LABOUR HERE.
ICE CREAM! ROASTED CHESTNUTS!
BAGHDAD BAZAAR
SUMMER GOODS
WINTER GOODS

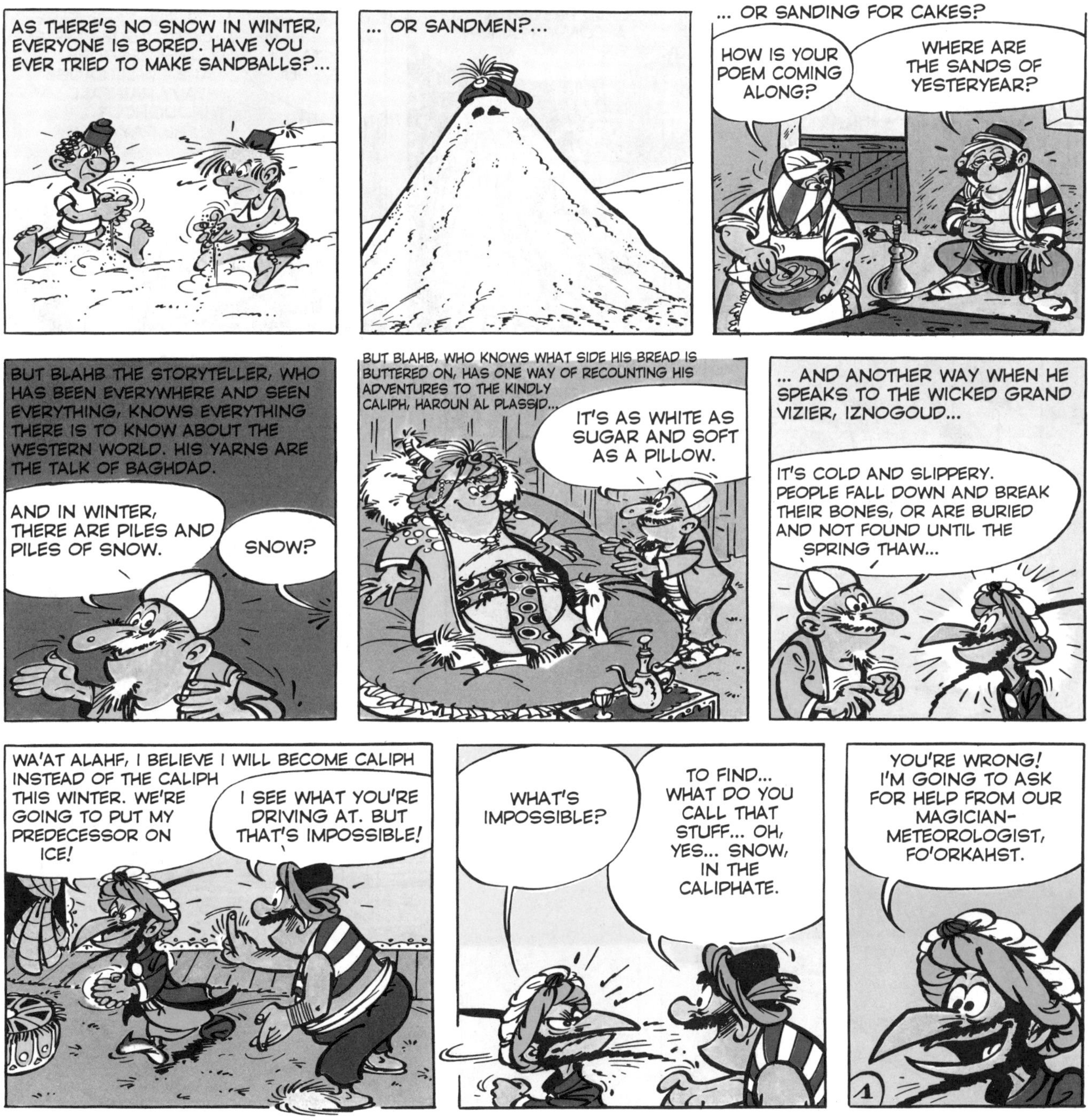

AS THERE'S NO SNOW IN WINTER, EVERYONE IS BORED. HAVE YOU EVER TRIED TO MAKE SANDBALLS?...
... OR SANDMEN?...
... OR SANDING FOR CAKES?
HOW IS YOUR POEM COMING ALONG?
WHERE ARE THE SANDS OF YESTERYEAR?
BUT BLAHB THE STORYTELLER, WHO HAS BEEN EVERYWHERE AND SEEN EVERYTHING, KNOWS EVERYTHING THERE IS TO KNOW ABOUT THE WESTERN WORLD. HIS YARNS ARE THE TALK OF BAGHDAD.
AND IN WINTER, THERE ARE PILES AND PILES OF SNOW.
SNOW?
BUT BLAHB, WHO KNOWS WHAT SIDE HIS BREAD IS BUTTERED ON, HAS ONE WAY OF RECOUNTING HIS ADVENTURES TO THE KINDLY CALIPH, HAROUN AL PLASSID...
IT'S AS WHITE AS SUGAR AND SOFT AS A PILLOW.
... AND ANOTHER WAY WHEN HE SPEAKS TO THE WICKED GRAND VIZIER, IZNOGOUD...
IT'S COLD AND SLIPPERY. PEOPLE FALL DOWN AND BREAK THEIR BONES, OR ARE BURIED AND NOT FOUND UNTIL THE SPRING THAW...
WA'AT ALAHF, I BELIEVE I WILL BECOME CALIPH INSTEAD OF THE CALIPH THIS WINTER. WE'RE GOING TO PUT MY PREDECESSOR ON ICE!
I SEE WHAT YOU'RE DRIVING AT. BUT THAT'S IMPOSSIBLE!
WHAT'S IMPOSSIBLE?
TO FIND... WHAT DO YOU CALL THAT STUFF... OH, YES... SNOW, IN THE CALIPHATE.
YOU'RE WRONG! I'M GOING TO ASK FOR HELP FROM OUR MAGICIAN-METEOROLOGIST, FO'ORKAHST.
1

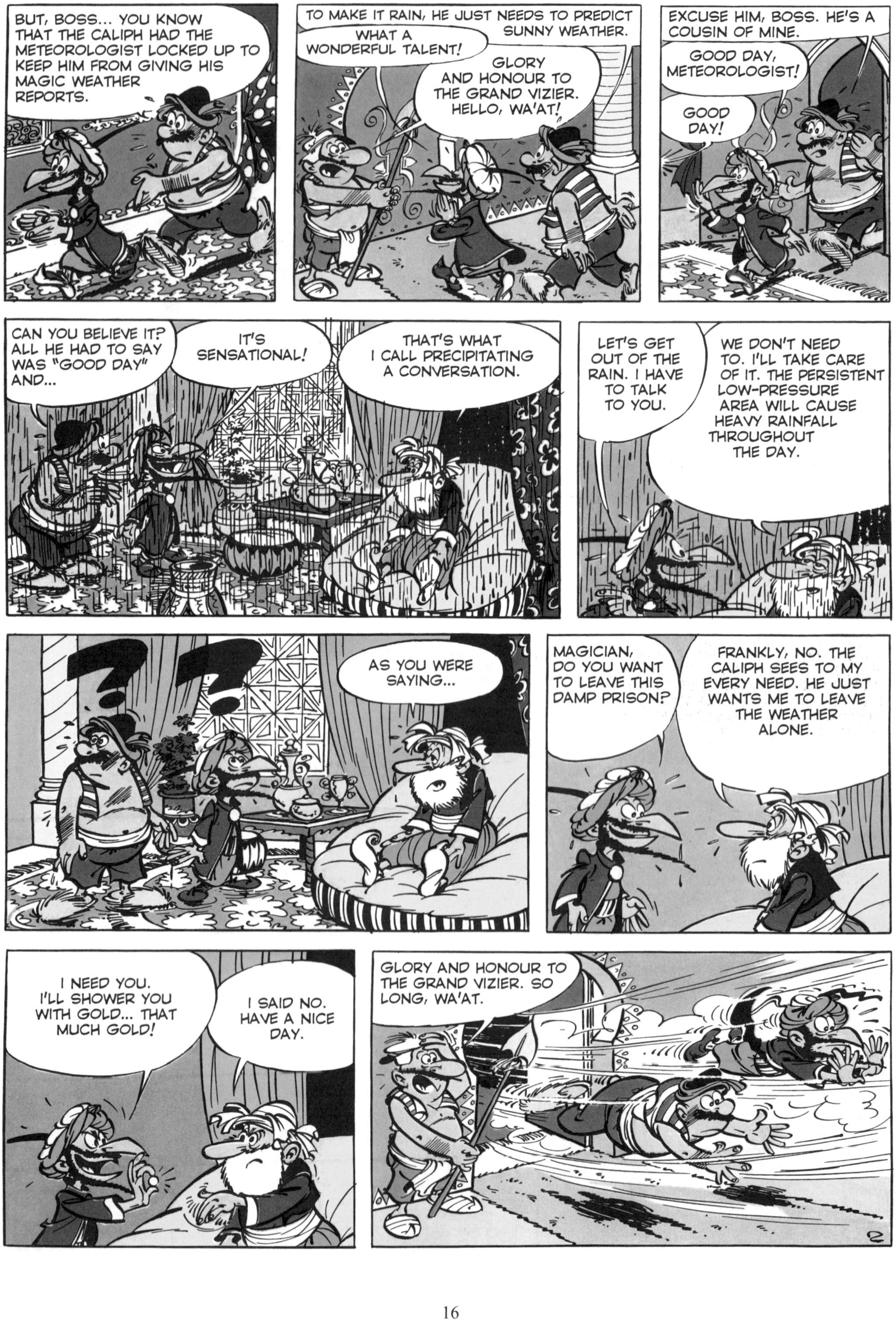

BUT, BOSS... YOU KNOW THAT THE CALIPH HAD THE METEOROLOGIST LOCKED UP TO KEEP HIM FROM GIVING HIS MAGIC WEATHER REPORTS.
TO MAKE IT RAIN, HE JUST NEEDS TO PREDICT SUNNY WEATHER.
WHAT A WONDERFUL TALENT!
GLORY AND HONOUR TO THE GRAND VIZIER. HELLO, WA'AT!
EXCUSE HIM, BOSS. HE'S A COUSIN OF MINE.
GOOD DAY, METEOROLOGIST!
GOOD DAY!
CAN YOU BELIEVE IT? ALL HE HAD TO SAY WAS "GOOD DAY" AND...
IT'S SENSATIONAL!
THAT'S WHAT I CALL PRECIPITATING A CONVERSATION.
LET'S GET OUT OF THE RAIN. I HAVE TO TALK TO YOU.
WE DON'T NEED TO. I'LL TAKE CARE OF IT. THE PERSISTENT LOW-PRESSURE AREA WILL CAUSE HEAVY RAINFALL THROUGHOUT THE DAY.
AS YOU WERE SAYING...
MAGICIAN, DO YOU WANT TO LEAVE THIS DAMP PRISON?
FRANKLY, NO. THE CALIPH SEES TO MY EVERY NEED. HE JUST WANTS ME TO LEAVE THE WEATHER ALONE.
I NEED YOU. I'LL SHOWER YOU WITH GOLD... THAT MUCH GOLD!
I SAID NO. HAVE A NICE DAY.
GLORY AND HONOUR TO THE GRAND VIZIER. SO LONG, WA'AT.

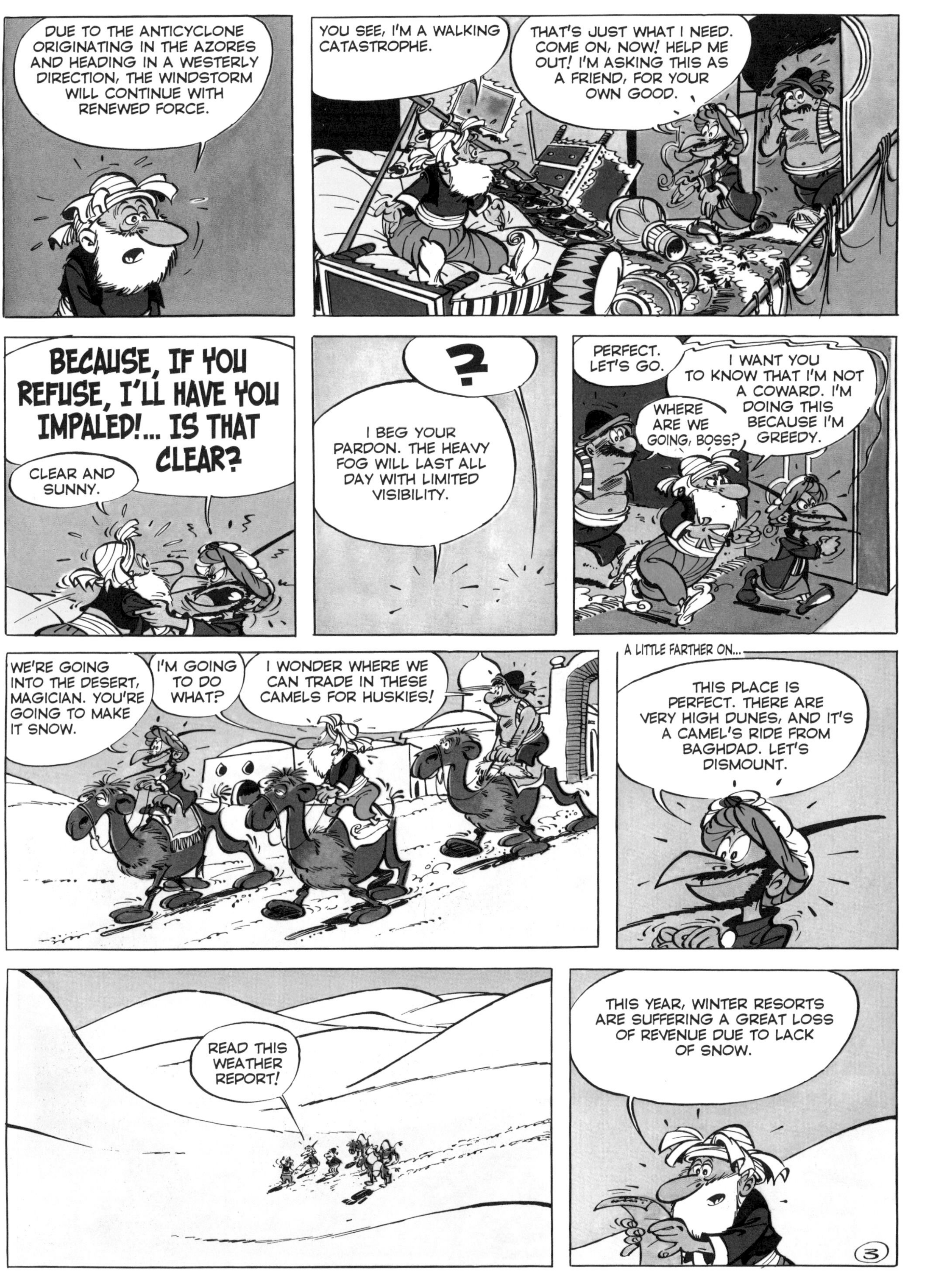
DUE TO THE ANTICYCLONE ORIGINATING IN THE AZORES AND HEADING IN A WESTERLY DIRECTION, THE WINDSTORM WILL CONTINUE WITH RENEWED FORCE.
YOU SEE, I'M A WALKING CATASTROPHE.
THAT'S JUST WHAT I NEED. COME ON, NOW! HELP ME OUT! I'M ASKING THIS AS A FRIEND, FOR YOUR OWN GOOD.
BECAUSE, IF YOU REFUSE, I'LL HAVE YOU IMPALED!... IS THAT CLEAR?
CLEAR AND SUNNY.
?
I BEG YOUR PARDON. THE HEAVY FOG WILL LAST ALL DAY WITH LIMITED VISIBILITY.
PERFECT. LET'S GO.
I WANT YOU TO KNOW THAT I'M NOT A COWARD. I'M DOING THIS BECAUSE I'M GREEDY.
WHERE ARE WE GOING, BOSS?
WE'RE GOING INTO THE DESERT, MAGICIAN. YOU'RE GOING TO MAKE IT SNOW.
I'M GOING TO DO WHAT?
I WONDER WHERE WE CAN TRADE IN THESE CAMELS FOR HUSKIES!
A LITTLE FARTHER ON...
THIS PLACE IS PERFECT. THERE ARE VERY HIGH DUNES, AND IT'S A CAMEL'S RIDE FROM BAGHDAD. LET'S DISMOUNT.
READ THIS WEATHER REPORT!
THIS YEAR, WINTER RESORTS ARE SUFFERING A GREAT LOSS OF REVENUE DUE TO LACK OF SNOW.
3

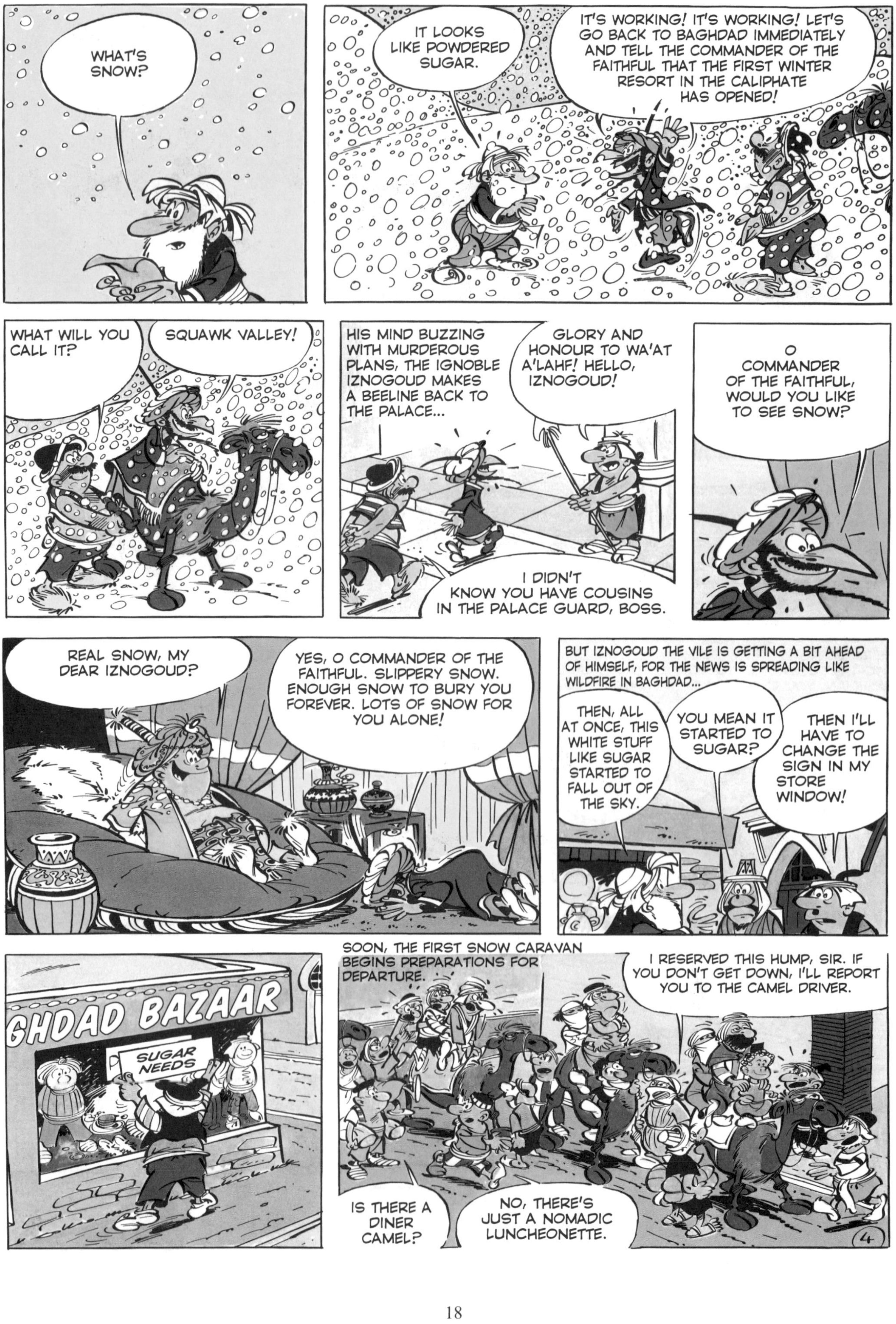
WHAT'S SNOW?
IT LOOKS LIKE POWDERED SUGAR.
IT'S WORKING! IT'S WORKING! LET'S GO BACK TO BAGHDAD IMMEDIATELY AND TELL THE COMMANDER OF THE FAITHFUL THAT THE FIRST WINTER RESORT IN THE CALIPHATE HAS OPENED!
WHAT WILL YOU CALL IT?
SQUAWK VALLEY!
HIS MIND BUZZING WITH MURDEROUS PLANS, THE IGNOBLE IZNOGOUD MAKES A BEELINE BACK TO THE PALACE...
GLORY AND HONOUR TO WA'AT A'LAHF! HELLO, IZNOGOUD!
I DIDN'T KNOW YOU HAVE COUSINS IN THE PALACE GUARD, BOSS.
O COMMANDER OF THE FAITHFUL, WOULD YOU LIKE TO SEE SNOW?
REAL SNOW, MY DEAR IZNOGOUD?
YES, O COMMANDER OF THE FAITHFUL. SLIPPERY SNOW. ENOUGH SNOW TO BURY YOU FOREVER. LOTS OF SNOW FOR YOU ALONE!
BUT IZNOGOUD THE VILE IS GETTING A BIT AHEAD OF HIMSELF, FOR THE NEWS IS SPREADING LIKE WILDFIRE IN BAGHDAD...
THEN, ALL AT ONCE, THIS WHITE STUFF LIKE SUGAR STARTED TO FALL OUT OF THE SKY.
YOU MEAN IT STARTED TO SUGAR?
THEN I'LL HAVE TO CHANGE THE SIGN IN MY STORE WINDOW!
GHDAD BAZAAR
SUGAR NEEDS
SOON, THE FIRST SNOW CARAVAN BEGINS PREPARATIONS FOR DEPARTURE.
I RESERVED THIS HUMP, SIR. IF YOU DON'T GET DOWN, I'LL REPORT YOU TO THE CAMEL DRIVER.
IS THERE A DINER CAMEL?
NO, THERE'S JUST A NOMADIC LUNCHEONETTE.
4

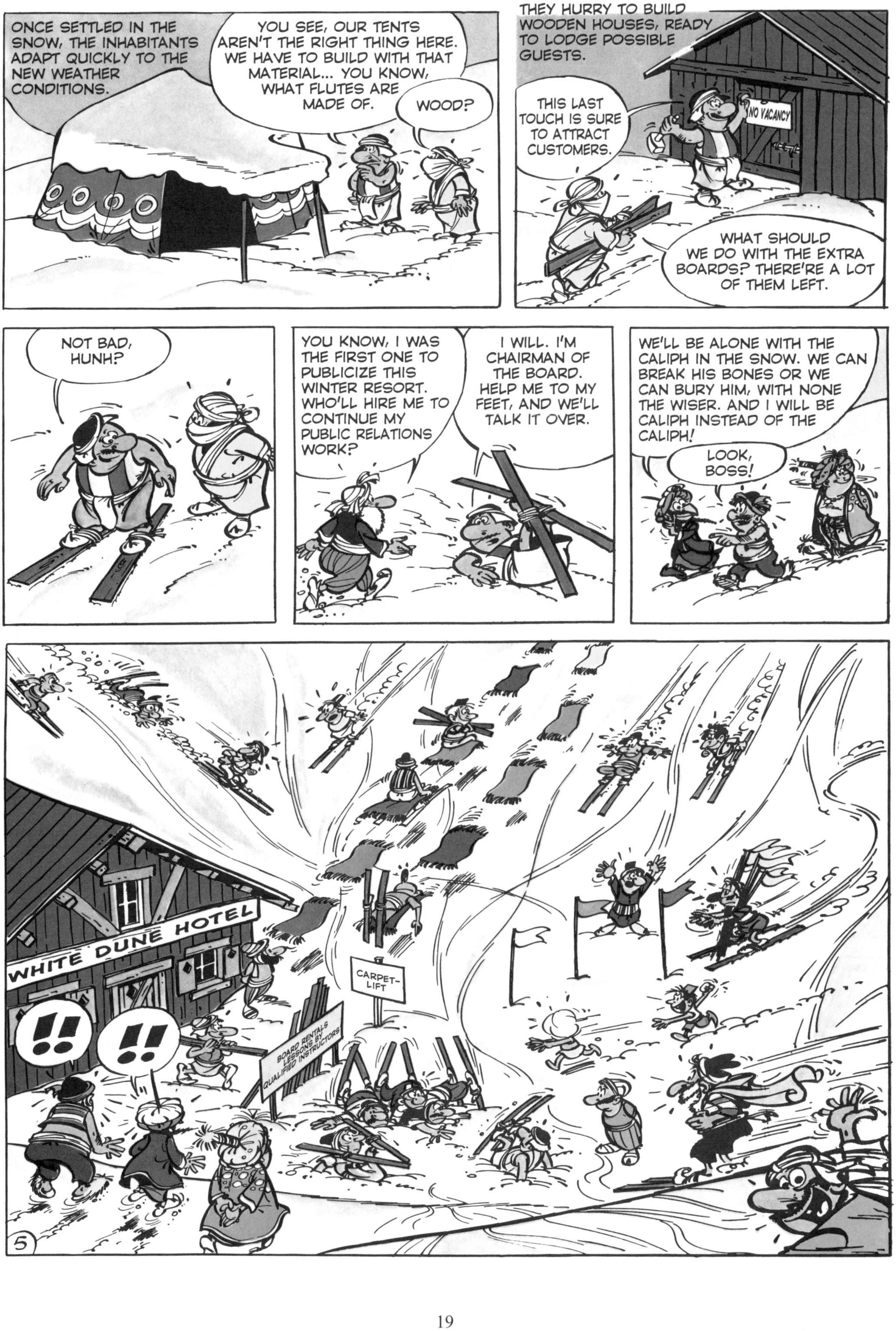
ONCE SETTLED IN THE SNOW, THE INHABITANTS ADAPT QUICKLY TO THE NEW WEATHER CONDITIONS.
YOU SEE, OUR TENTS AREN'T THE RIGHT THING HERE. WE HAVE TO BUILD WITH THAT MATERIAL... YOU KNOW, WHAT FLUTES ARE MADE OF.
WOOD?
THEY HURRY TO BUILD WOODEN HOUSES, READY TO LODGE POSSIBLE GUESTS.
THIS LAST TOUCH IS SURE TO ATTRACT CUSTOMERS.
NO VACANCY
WHAT SHOULD WE DO WITH THE EXTRA BOARDS? THERE'RE A LOT OF THEM LEFT.
NOT BAD, HUNH?
YOU KNOW, I WAS THE FIRST ONE TO PUBLICIZE THIS WINTER RESORT. WHO'LL HIRE ME TO CONTINUE MY PUBLIC RELATIONS WORK?
I WILL. I'M CHAIRMAN OF THE BOARD. HELP ME TO MY FEET, AND WE'LL TALK IT OVER.
WE'LL BE ALONE WITH THE CALIPH IN THE SNOW. WE CAN BREAK HIS BONES OR WE CAN BURY HIM, WITH NONE THE WISER. AND I WILL BE CALIPH INSTEAD OF THE CALIPH!
LOOK, BOSS!
WHITE DUNE HOTEL
CARPET-LIFT
BOARD RENTALS
LESSONS BY QUALIFIED INSTRUCTORS
!!
!!

THERE'S QUITE A CROWD HERE!
WE'LL FIND A LONELY SPOT TO, UH... LET THAT SLIDE BY. WE'LL RENT BOARDS FOR YOU.
THAT'S VERY NICE OF YOU, MY DEAR IZNOGOUD. BUT I DON'T KNOW HOW TO USE THEM...
IT'S EASY AND FUN. YOU WON'T BE BORED.
EASY? REALLY?
I PICKED OUT A BUMP ON THE SLOPE. I'LL AIM HIM TOWARDS IT AND—ALLEY OOP! I'LL BE CALIPH INSTEAD OF THE CALIPH!
BOSS, BELIEVE ME: SOMEHOW WE'LL HAVE COLD WATER THROWN ON OUR PLANS! AS USUAL...
BUT I'M NOT BRAVE ENOUGH, MY DEAR IZNOGOUD!
I'LL GIVE YOU A LITTLE...
...HELP!
IT'S NICE OF YOU TO COME WITH ME, IZNOGOUD.
DON'T TURN AROUND!
6

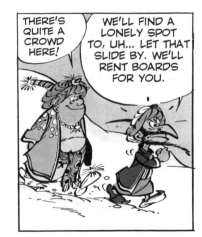

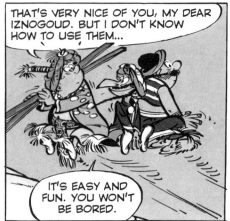

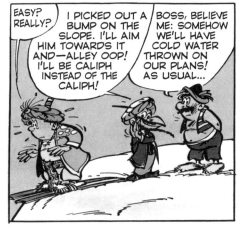

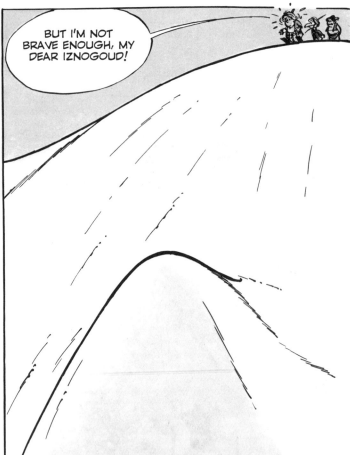

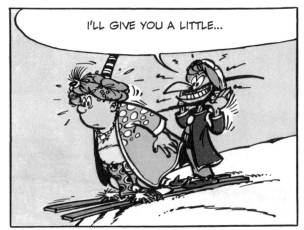

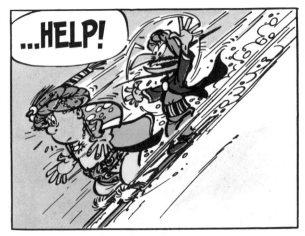

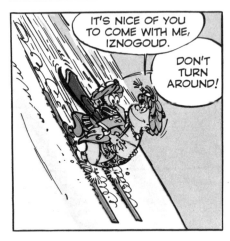

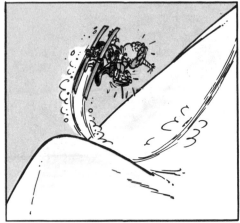

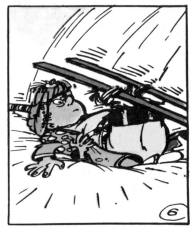

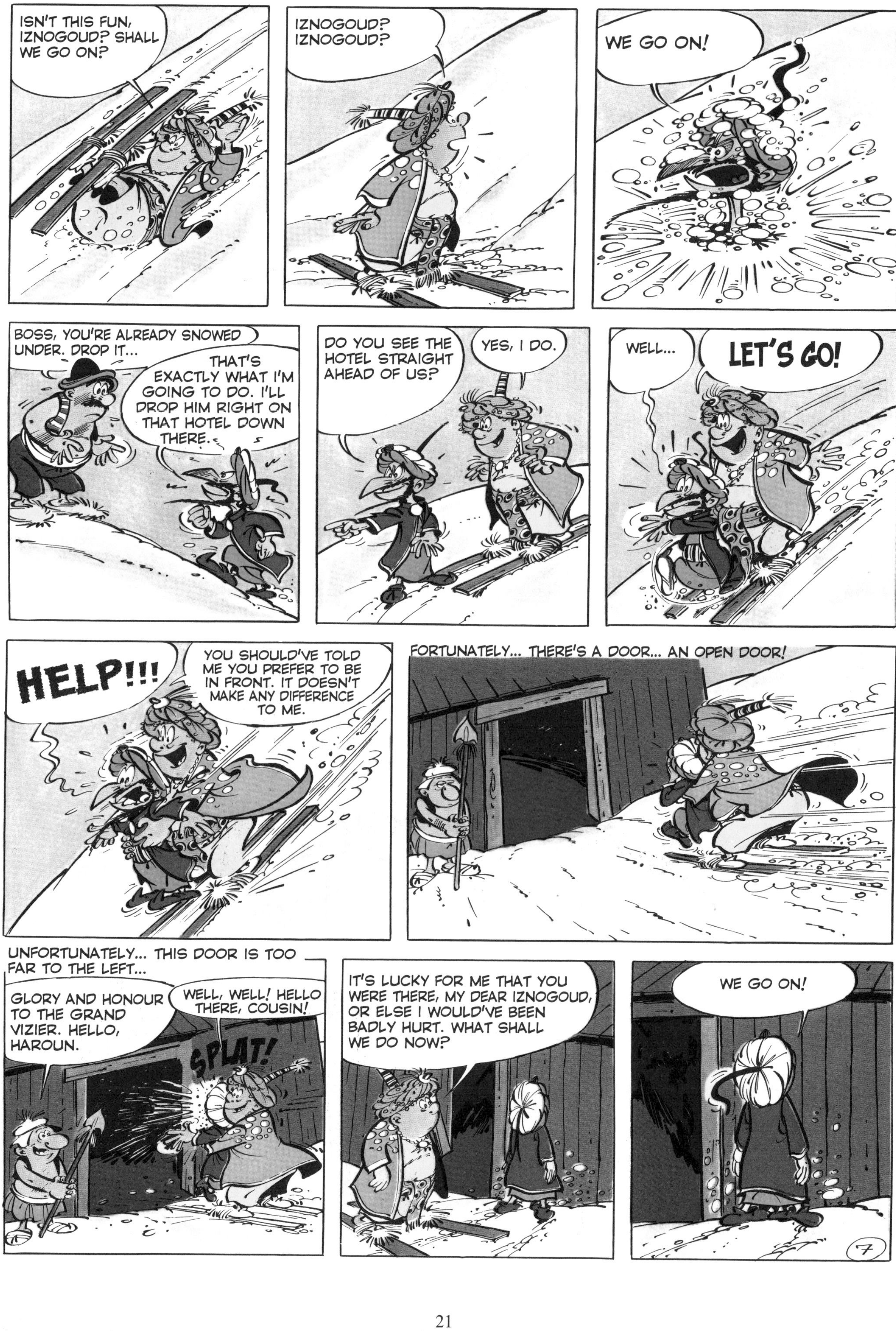
ISN'T THIS FUN, IZNOGOUD? SHALL WE GO ON?
IZNOGOUD? IZNOGOUD?
WE GO ON!
BOSS, YOU'RE ALREADY SNOWED UNDER. DROP IT...
THAT'S EXACTLY WHAT I'M GOING TO DO. I'LL DROP HIM RIGHT ON THAT HOTEL DOWN THERE.
DO YOU SEE THE HOTEL STRAIGHT AHEAD OF US?
YES, I DO.
WELL...
LET'S GO!
HELP!!!
YOU SHOULD'VE TOLD ME YOU PREFER TO BE IN FRONT. IT DOESN'T MAKE ANY DIFFERENCE TO ME.
FORTUNATELY... THERE'S A DOOR... AN OPEN DOOR!
UNFORTUNATELY... THIS DOOR IS TOO FAR TO THE LEFT...
GLORY AND HONOUR TO THE GRAND VIZIER. HELLO, HAROUN.
WELL, WELL! HELLO THERE, COUSIN!
SPLAT!
IT'S LUCKY FOR ME THAT YOU WERE THERE, MY DEAR IZNOGOUD, OR ELSE I WOULD'VE BEEN BADLY HURT. WHAT SHALL WE DO NOW?
WE GO ON!
7

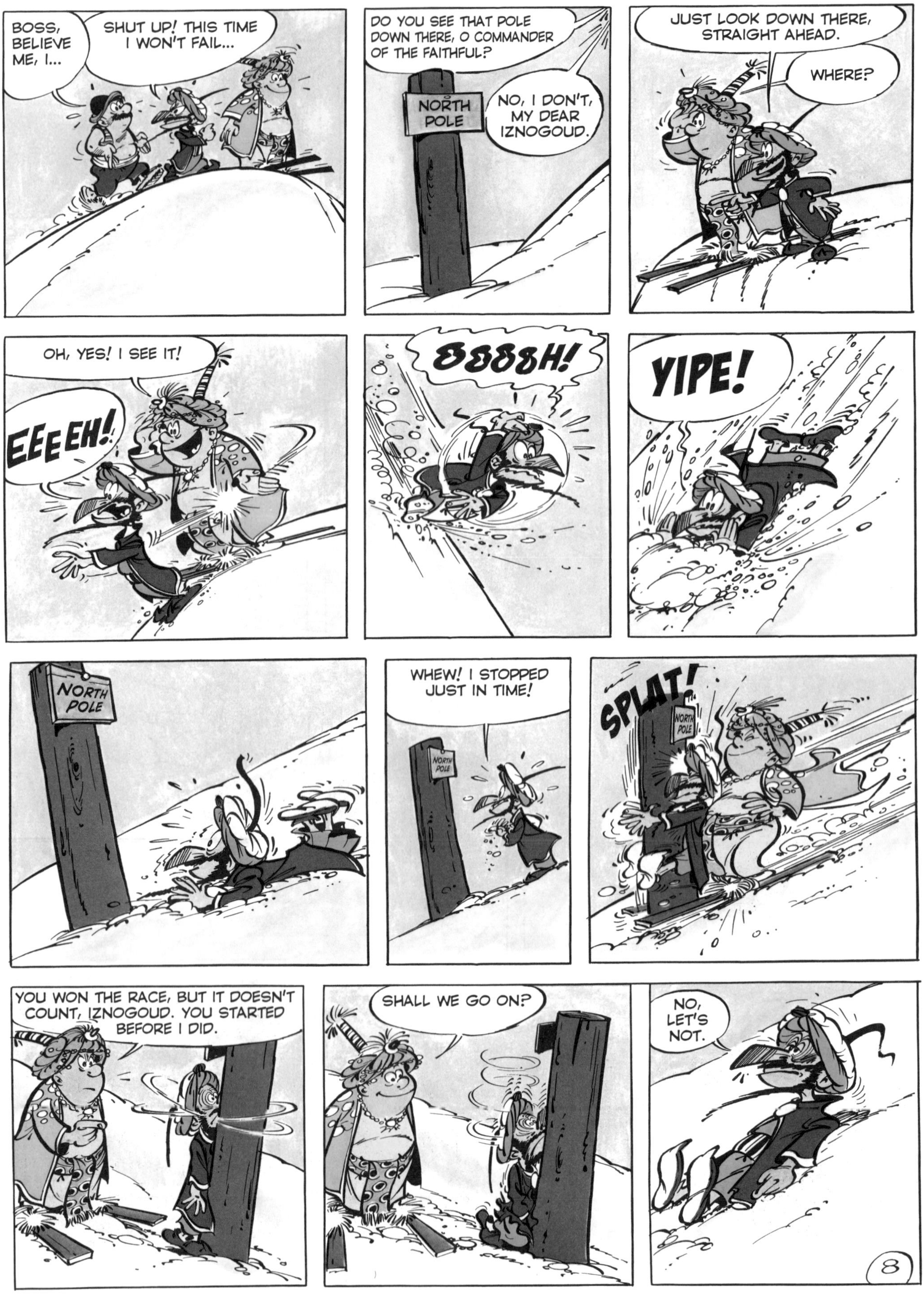

BOSS, BELIEVE ME, I...
SHUT UP! THIS TIME I WON'T FAIL...
DO YOU SEE THAT POLE DOWN THERE, O COMMANDER OF THE FAITHFUL?
NORTH POLE
NO, I DON'T, MY DEAR IZNOGOUD.
JUST LOOK DOWN THERE, STRAIGHT AHEAD.
WHERE?
OH, YES! I SEE IT!
EEEEH!
8888H!
YIPE!
NORTH POLE
WHEW! I STOPPED JUST IN TIME!
NORTH POLE
SPLAT!
NORTH POLE
YOU WON THE RACE, BUT IT DOESN'T COUNT, IZNOGOUD. YOU STARTED BEFORE I DID.
SHALL WE GO ON?
NO, LET'S NOT.
8

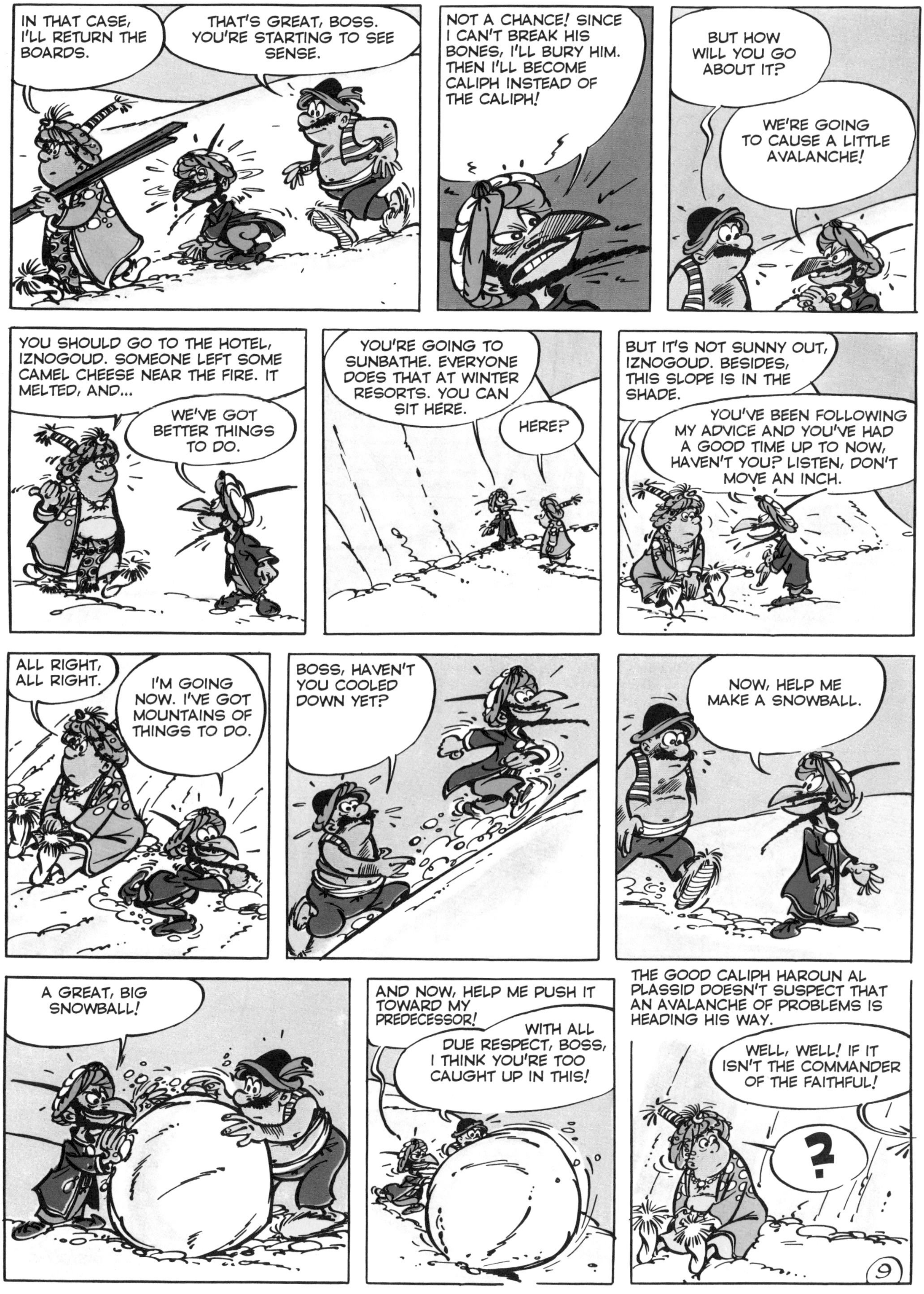
IN THAT CASE, I'LL RETURN THE BOARDS.
THAT'S GREAT, BOSS. YOU'RE STARTING TO SEE SENSE.
NOT A CHANCE! SINCE I CAN'T BREAK HIS BONES, I'LL BURY HIM. THEN I'LL BECOME CALIPH INSTEAD OF THE CALIPH!
BUT HOW WILL YOU GO ABOUT IT?
WE'RE GOING TO CAUSE A LITTLE AVALANCHE!
YOU SHOULD GO TO THE HOTEL, IZNOGOUD. SOMEONE LEFT SOME CAMEL CHEESE NEAR THE FIRE. IT MELTED, AND...
WE'VE GOT BETTER THINGS TO DO.
YOU'RE GOING TO SUNBATHE. EVERYONE DOES THAT AT WINTER RESORTS. YOU CAN SIT HERE.
HERE?
BUT IT'S NOT SUNNY OUT, IZNOGOUD. BESIDES, THIS SLOPE IS IN THE SHADE.
YOU'VE BEEN FOLLOWING MY ADVICE AND YOU'VE HAD A GOOD TIME UP TO NOW, HAVEN'T YOU? LISTEN, DON'T MOVE AN INCH.
ALL RIGHT, ALL RIGHT.
I'M GOING NOW. I'VE GOT MOUNTAINS OF THINGS TO DO.
BOSS, HAVEN'T YOU COOLED DOWN YET?
NOW, HELP ME MAKE A SNOWBALL.
A GREAT, BIG SNOWBALL!
AND NOW, HELP ME PUSH IT TOWARD MY PREDECESSOR!
WITH ALL DUE RESPECT, BOSS, I THINK YOU'RE TOO CAUGHT UP IN THIS!
THE GOOD CALIPH HAROUN AL PLASSID DOESN'T SUSPECT THAT AN AVALANCHE OF PROBLEMS IS HEADING HIS WAY.
WELL, WELL! IF IT ISN'T THE COMMANDER OF THE FAITHFUL!
?
9

WELL, WELL! IF IT ISN'T THE METEOROLOGIST!? I TOLD YOU TO STAY IN YOUR QUARTERS!

YOU DID, BUT I DON'T MAKE WEATHER FORECASTS ANYMORE, O COMMANDER OF THE FAITHFUL.

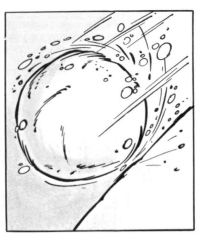

I'M DIRECTOR OF THIS RESORT'S CHAMBER OF COMMERCE, YOU SEE.

THAT'S GOOD NEWS.

SO, YOU MUST BE ON TOP OF EVERYTHING. DO YOU THINK WE'LL HAVE MORE COLD WEATHER AND SNOW?

LIKE THE GOOD DIRECTOR OF THE CHAMBER OF COMMERCE THAT HE IS, FO'ORKAHST ANSWERS...

YES, OF COURSE!

NATURALLY, THIS ANSWER CAUSES AN IMMEDIATE CHANGE IN THE WEATHER... THE MOST TORRID HEAT WAVE EVER FELT IN THIS PART OF THE DESERT.

METEOROLOGIST, YOU'RE IMPOSSIBLE. I'M GOING BACK WITH YOU TO THE PALACE AND MAKE SURE YOU DON'T GET INTO ANY MORE TROUBLE.

AH, YES. ONCE AGAIN, THE GRAND VIZIER IZNOGOUD AND HIS EVIL PLANS ARE LEFT HIGH AND DRY.

BOSS, I TOLD YOU OUR PLANS WOULD GO UP IN SMOKE.

SCRIPT: GOSCINNY   DRAWING: TABARY-66

THE CALIPH'S CRUISE

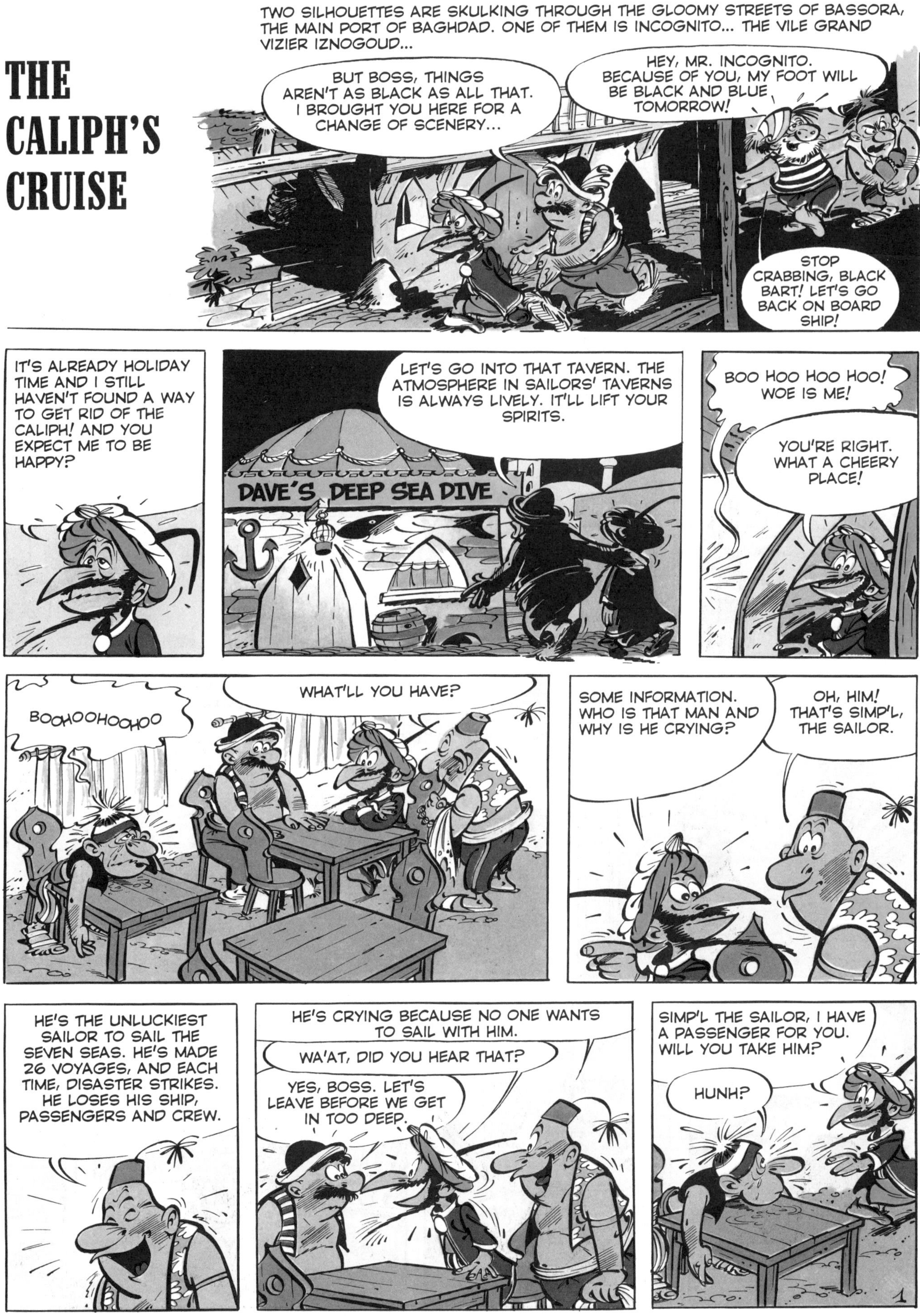

TWO SILHOUETTES ARE SKULKING THROUGH THE GLOOMY STREETS OF BASSORA, THE MAIN PORT OF BAGHDAD. ONE OF THEM IS INCOGNITO... THE VILE GRAND VIZIER IZNOGOUD...
BUT BOSS, THINGS AREN'T AS BLACK AS ALL THAT. I BROUGHT YOU HERE FOR A CHANGE OF SCENERY...
HEY, MR. INCOGNITO. BECAUSE OF YOU, MY FOOT WILL BE BLACK AND BLUE TOMORROW!
STOP CRABBING, BLACK BART! LET'S GO BACK ON BOARD SHIP!
IT'S ALREADY HOLIDAY TIME AND I STILL HAVEN'T FOUND A WAY TO GET RID OF THE CALIPH! AND YOU EXPECT ME TO BE HAPPY?
LET'S GO INTO THAT TAVERN. THE ATMOSPHERE IN SAILORS' TAVERNS IS ALWAYS LIVELY. IT'LL LIFT YOUR SPIRITS.
DAVE'S DEEP SEA DIVE
BOO HOO HOO HOO! WOE IS ME!
YOU'RE RIGHT. WHAT A CHEERY PLACE!
BOOHOOHOOHOO
WHAT'LL YOU HAVE?
SOME INFORMATION. WHO IS THAT MAN AND WHY IS HE CRYING?
OH, HIM! THAT'S SIMP'L, THE SAILOR.
HE'S THE UNLUCKIEST SAILOR TO SAIL THE SEVEN SEAS. HE'S MADE 26 VOYAGES, AND EACH TIME, DISASTER STRIKES. HE LOSES HIS SHIP, PASSENGERS AND CREW.
HE'S CRYING BECAUSE NO ONE WANTS TO SAIL WITH HIM.
WA'AT, DID YOU HEAR THAT?
YES, BOSS. LET'S LEAVE BEFORE WE GET IN TOO DEEP.
SIMP'L THE SAILOR, I HAVE A PASSENGER FOR YOU. WILL YOU TAKE HIM?
HUNH?
1

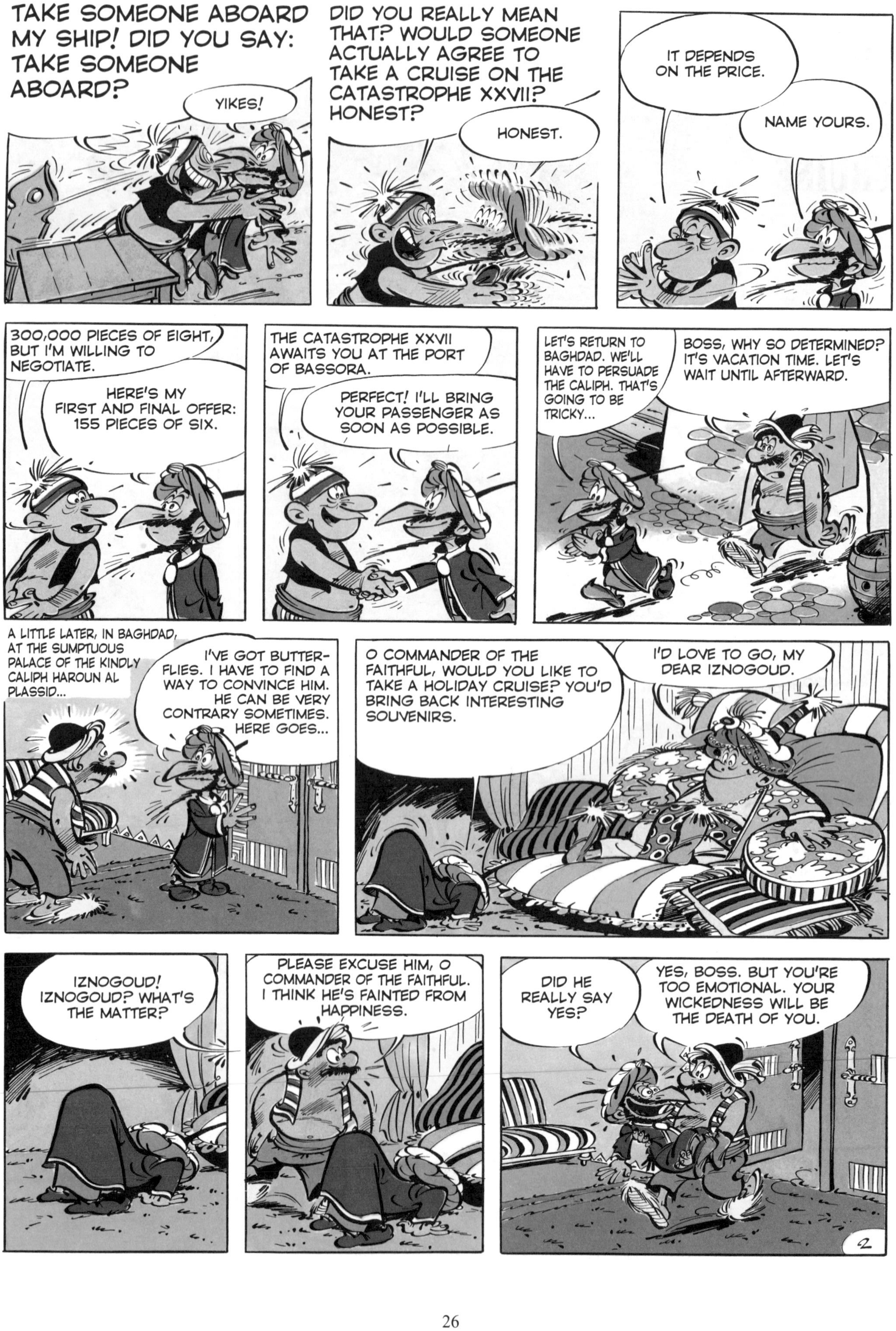

TAKE SOMEONE ABOARD MY SHIP! DID YOU SAY: TAKE SOMEONE ABOARD?
YIKES!
DID YOU REALLY MEAN THAT? WOULD SOMEONE ACTUALLY AGREE TO TAKE A CRUISE ON THE CATASTROPHE XXVII? HONEST?
HONEST.
IT DEPENDS ON THE PRICE.
NAME YOURS.
300,000 PIECES OF EIGHT, BUT I'M WILLING TO NEGOTIATE.
HERE'S MY FIRST AND FINAL OFFER: 155 PIECES OF SIX.
THE CATASTROPHE XXVII AWAITS YOU AT THE PORT OF BASSORA.
PERFECT! I'LL BRING YOUR PASSENGER AS SOON AS POSSIBLE.
LET'S RETURN TO BAGHDAD. WE'LL HAVE TO PERSUADE THE CALIPH. THAT'S GOING TO BE TRICKY...
BOSS, WHY SO DETERMINED? IT'S VACATION TIME. LET'S WAIT UNTIL AFTERWARD.
A LITTLE LATER, IN BAGHDAD, AT THE SUMPTUOUS PALACE OF THE KINDLY CALIPH HAROUN AL PLASSID...
I'VE GOT BUTTERFLIES. I HAVE TO FIND A WAY TO CONVINCE HIM. HE CAN BE VERY CONTRARY SOMETIMES. HERE GOES...
O COMMANDER OF THE FAITHFUL, WOULD YOU LIKE TO TAKE A HOLIDAY CRUISE? YOU'D BRING BACK INTERESTING SOUVENIRS.
I'D LOVE TO GO, MY DEAR IZNOGOUD.
IZNOGOUD! IZNOGOUD? WHAT'S THE MATTER?
PLEASE EXCUSE HIM, O COMMANDER OF THE FAITHFUL. I THINK HE'S FAINTED FROM HAPPINESS.
DID HE REALLY SAY YES?
YES, BOSS. BUT YOU'RE TOO EMOTIONAL. YOUR WICKEDNESS WILL BE THE DEATH OF YOU.
2

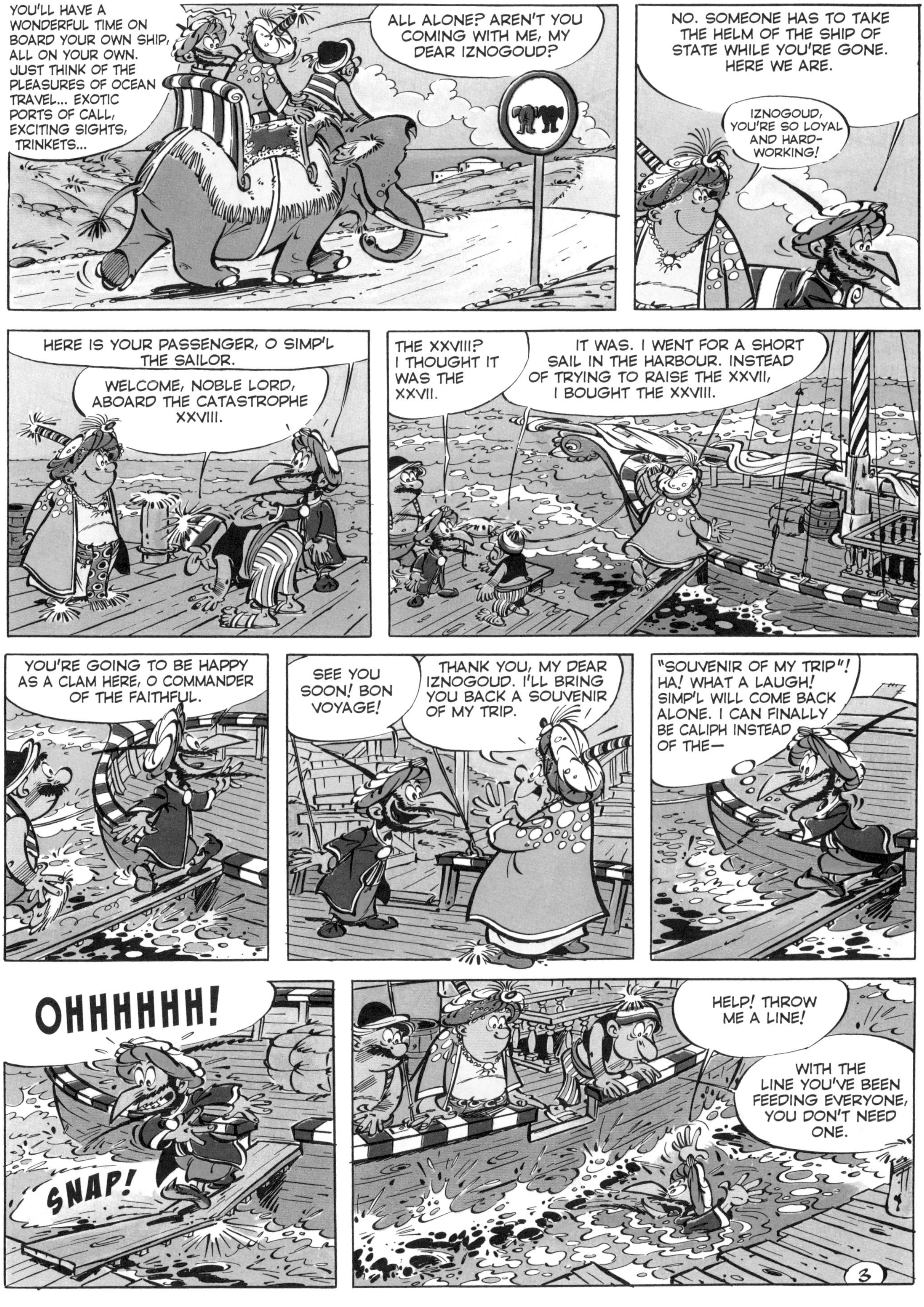
YOU'LL HAVE A WONDERFUL TIME ON BOARD YOUR OWN SHIP, ALL ON YOUR OWN. JUST THINK OF THE PLEASURES OF OCEAN TRAVEL... EXOTIC PORTS OF CALL, EXCITING SIGHTS, TRINKETS...
ALL ALONE? AREN'T YOU COMING WITH ME, MY DEAR IZNOGOUD?
NO. SOMEONE HAS TO TAKE THE HELM OF THE SHIP OF STATE WHILE YOU'RE GONE. HERE WE ARE.
IZNOGOUD, YOU'RE SO LOYAL AND HARD-WORKING!
HERE IS YOUR PASSENGER, O SIMP'L THE SAILOR.
WELCOME, NOBLE LORD, ABOARD THE CATASTROPHE XXVIII.
THE XXVIII? I THOUGHT IT WAS THE XXVII.
IT WAS. I WENT FOR A SHORT SAIL IN THE HARBOUR. INSTEAD OF TRYING TO RAISE THE XXVII, I BOUGHT THE XXVIII.
YOU'RE GOING TO BE HAPPY AS A CLAM HERE, O COMMANDER OF THE FAITHFUL.
SEE YOU SOON! BON VOYAGE!
THANK YOU, MY DEAR IZNOGOUD. I'LL BRING YOU BACK A SOUVENIR OF MY TRIP.
"SOUVENIR OF MY TRIP"! HA! WHAT A LAUGH! SIMP'L WILL COME BACK ALONE. I CAN FINALLY BE CALIPH INSTEAD OF THE—
OHHHHHH!
SNAP!
HELP! THROW ME A LINE!
WITH THE LINE YOU'VE BEEN FEEDING EVERYONE, YOU DON'T NEED ONE.
3

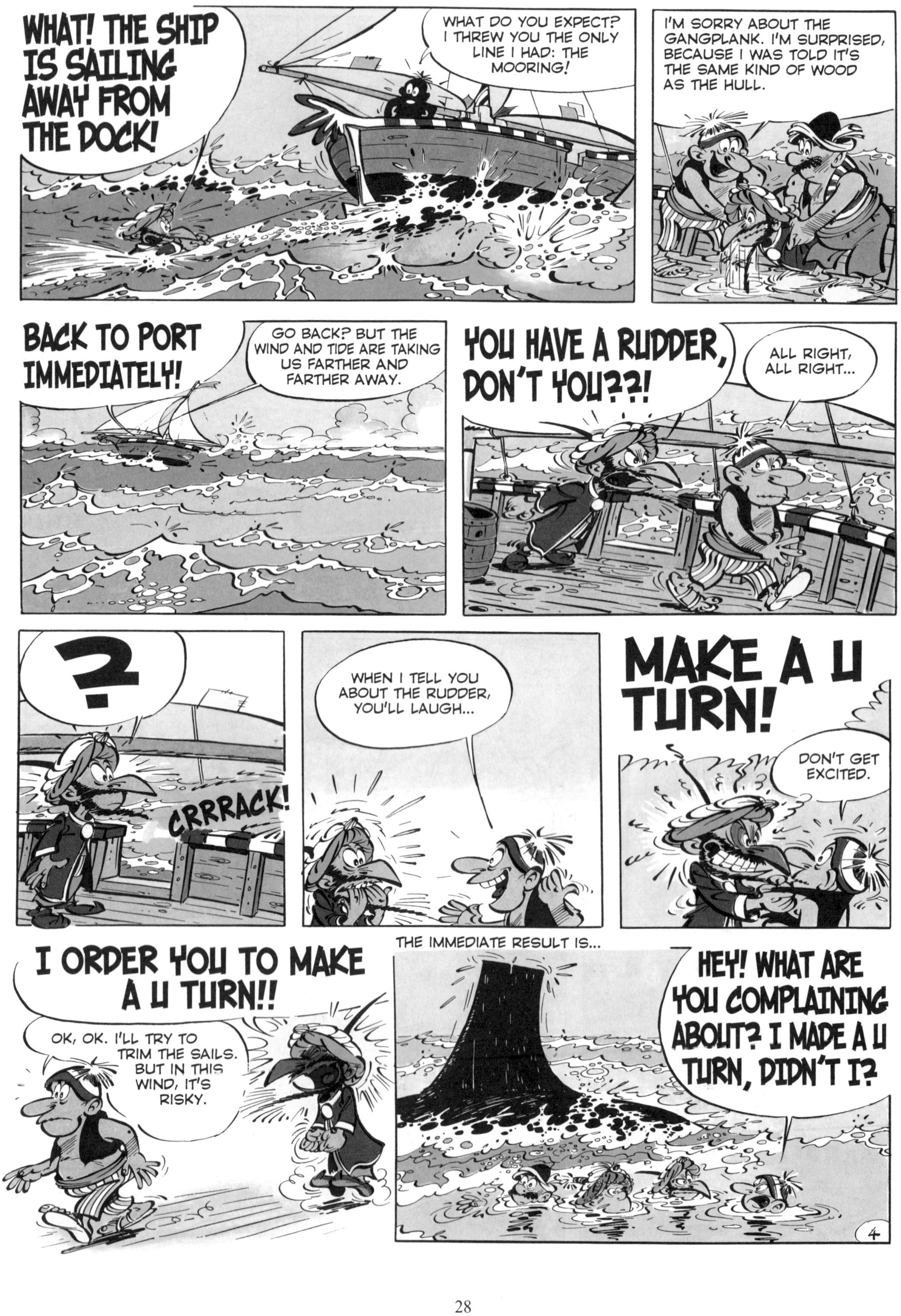
WHAT! THE SHIP IS SAILING AWAY FROM THE DOCK!
WHAT DO YOU EXPECT? I THREW YOU THE ONLY LINE I HAD: THE MOORING!
I'M SORRY ABOUT THE GANGPLANK. I'M SURPRISED, BECAUSE I WAS TOLD IT'S THE SAME KIND OF WOOD AS THE HULL.
BACK TO PORT IMMEDIATELY!
GO BACK? BUT THE WIND AND TIDE ARE TAKING US FARTHER AND FARTHER AWAY.
YOU HAVE A RUDDER, DON'T YOU??!
ALL RIGHT, ALL RIGHT...
?
CRRRACK!
WHEN I TELL YOU ABOUT THE RUDDER, YOU'LL LAUGH...
MAKE A U TURN!
DON'T GET EXCITED.
I ORDER YOU TO MAKE A U TURN!!
OK, OK. I'LL TRY TO TRIM THE SAILS. BUT IN THIS WIND, IT'S RISKY.
THE IMMEDIATE RESULT IS...
HEY! WHAT ARE YOU COMPLAINING ABOUT? I MADE A U TURN, DIDN'T I?
4

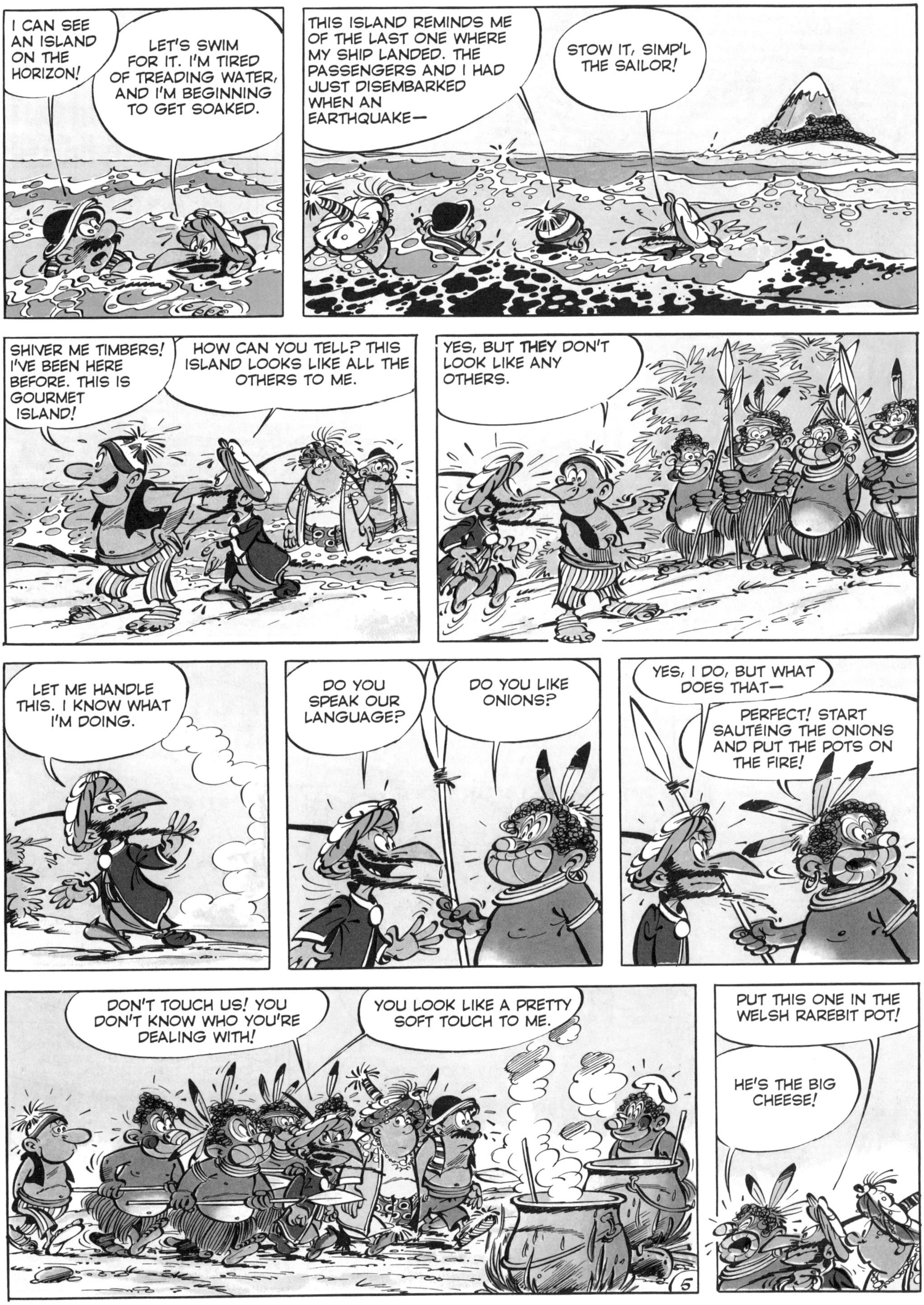
I CAN SEE AN ISLAND ON THE HORIZON!
LET'S SWIM FOR IT. I'M TIRED OF TREADING WATER, AND I'M BEGINNING TO GET SOAKED.
THIS ISLAND REMINDS ME OF THE LAST ONE WHERE MY SHIP LANDED. THE PASSENGERS AND I HAD JUST DISEMBARKED WHEN AN EARTHQUAKE—
STOW IT, SIMP'L THE SAILOR!
SHIVER ME TIMBERS! I'VE BEEN HERE BEFORE. THIS IS GOURMET ISLAND!
HOW CAN YOU TELL? THIS ISLAND LOOKS LIKE ALL THE OTHERS TO ME.
YES, BUT THEY DON'T LOOK LIKE ANY OTHERS.
LET ME HANDLE THIS. I KNOW WHAT I'M DOING.
DO YOU SPEAK OUR LANGUAGE?
DO YOU LIKE ONIONS?
YES, I DO, BUT WHAT DOES THAT—
PERFECT! START SAUTÉING THE ONIONS AND PUT THE POTS ON THE FIRE!
DON'T TOUCH US! YOU DON'T KNOW WHO YOU'RE DEALING WITH!
YOU LOOK LIKE A PRETTY SOFT TOUCH TO ME.
5
PUT THIS ONE IN THE WELSH RAREBIT POT!
HE'S THE BIG CHEESE!

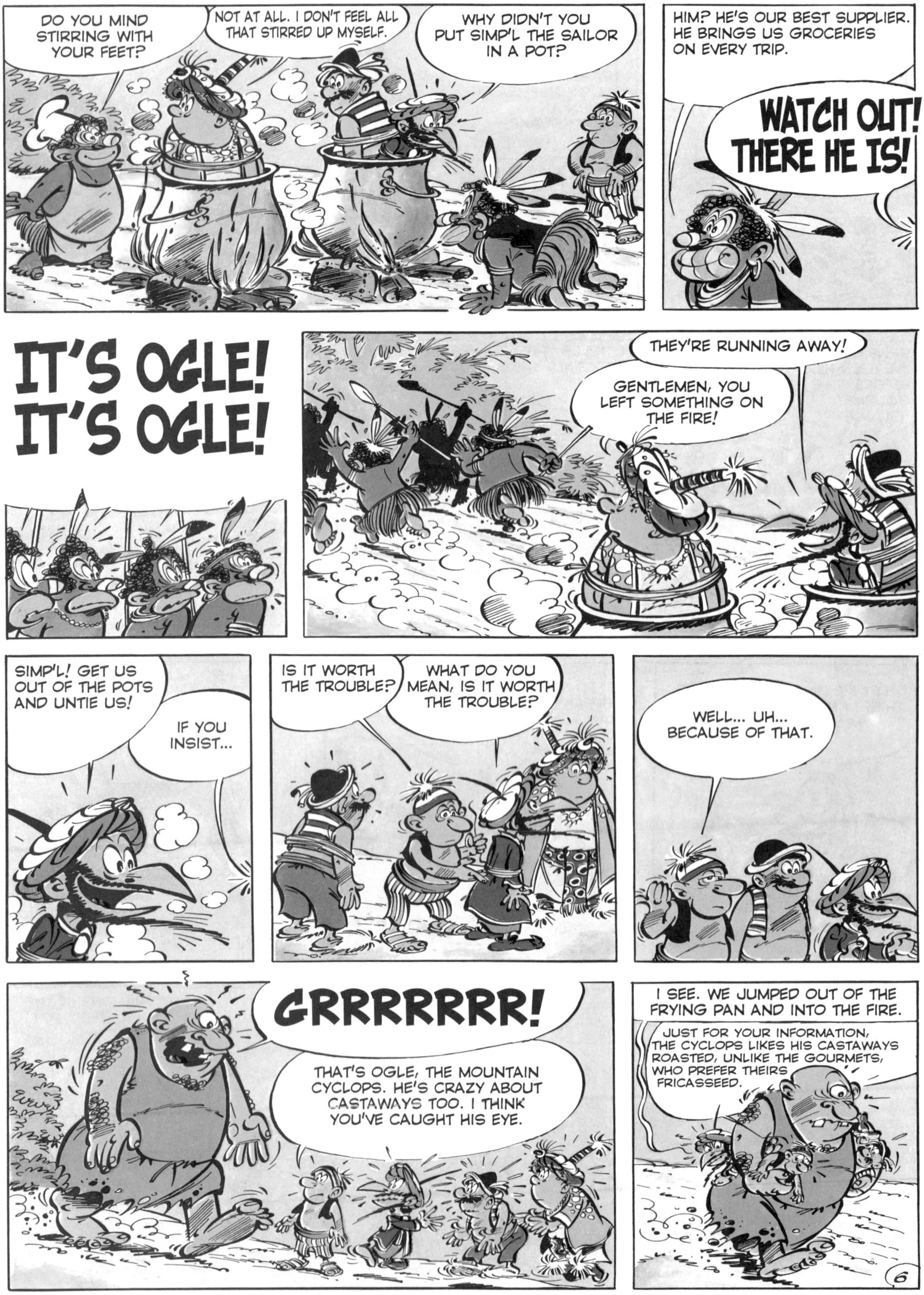
DO YOU MIND STIRRING WITH YOUR FEET?
NOT AT ALL. I DON'T FEEL ALL THAT STIRRED UP MYSELF.
WHY DIDN'T YOU PUT SIMP'L THE SAILOR IN A POT?
HIM? HE'S OUR BEST SUPPLIER. HE BRINGS US GROCERIES ON EVERY TRIP.
WATCH OUT! THERE HE IS!
IT'S OGLE! IT'S OGLE!
THEY'RE RUNNING AWAY!
GENTLEMEN, YOU LEFT SOMETHING ON THE FIRE!
SIMP'L! GET US OUT OF THE POTS AND UNTIE US!
IF YOU INSIST...
IS IT WORTH THE TROUBLE?
WHAT DO YOU MEAN, IS IT WORTH THE TROUBLE?
WELL... UH... BECAUSE OF THAT.
GRRRRRRR!
THAT'S OGLE, THE MOUNTAIN CYCLOPS. HE'S CRAZY ABOUT CASTAWAYS TOO. I THINK YOU'VE CAUGHT HIS EYE.
I SEE. WE JUMPED OUT OF THE FRYING PAN AND INTO THE FIRE.
JUST FOR YOUR INFORMATION, THE CYCLOPS LIKES HIS CASTAWAYS ROASTED, UNLIKE THE GOURMETS, WHO PREFER THEIRS FRICASSEED.
6

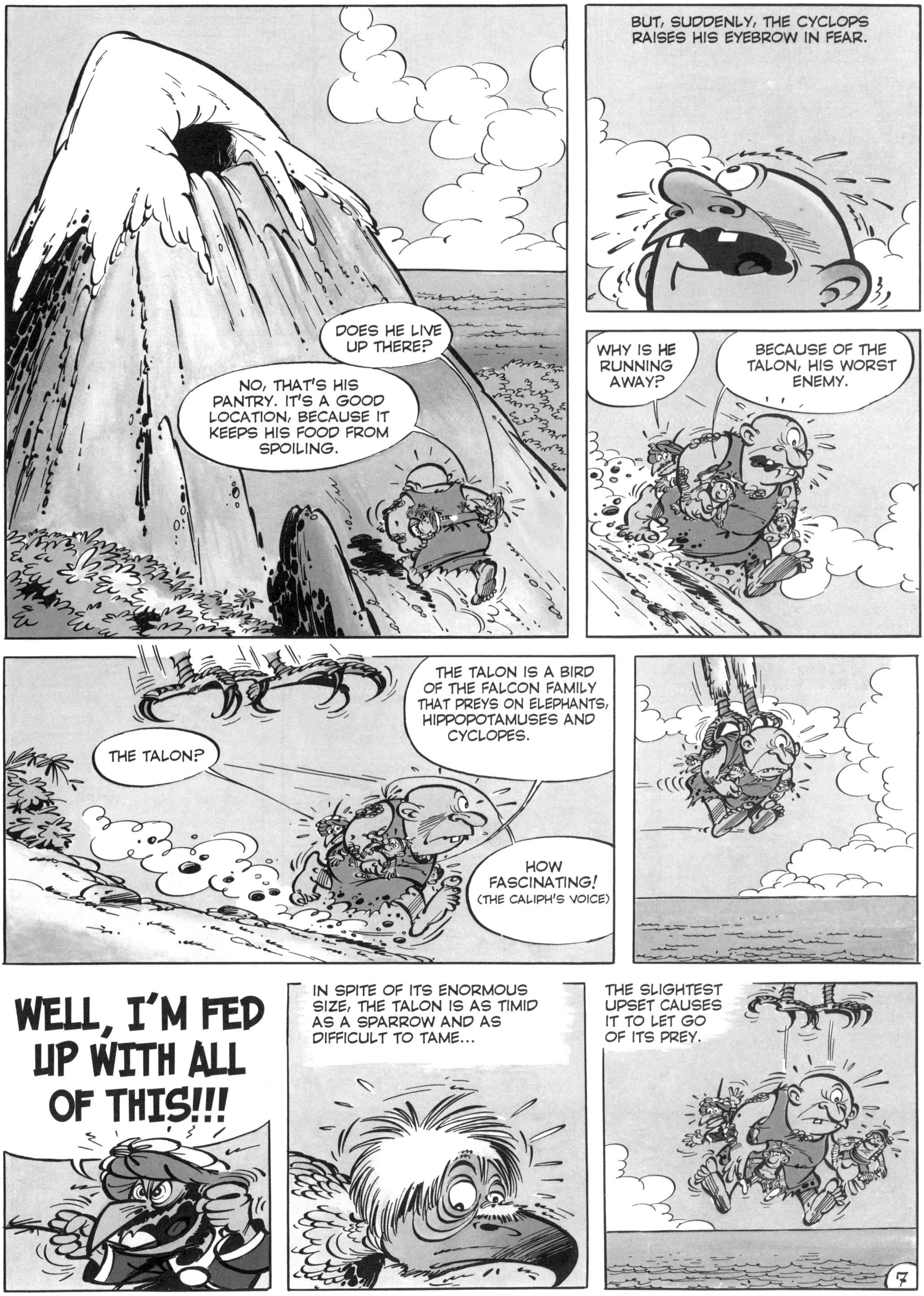
BUT, SUDDENLY, THE CYCLOPS RAISES HIS EYEBROW IN FEAR.
DOES HE LIVE UP THERE?
NO, THAT'S HIS PANTRY. IT'S A GOOD LOCATION, BECAUSE IT KEEPS HIS FOOD FROM SPOILING.
WHY IS HE RUNNING AWAY?
BECAUSE OF THE TALON, HIS WORST ENEMY.
THE TALON?
THE TALON IS A BIRD OF THE FALCON FAMILY THAT PREYS ON ELEPHANTS, HIPPOPOTAMUSES AND CYCLOPES.
HOW FASCINATING! (THE CALIPH'S VOICE)
WELL, I'M FED UP WITH ALL OF THIS!!!
IN SPITE OF ITS ENORMOUS SIZE, THE TALON IS AS TIMID AS A SPARROW AND AS DIFFICULT TO TAME...
THE SLIGHTEST UPSET CAUSES IT TO LET GO OF ITS PREY.
7

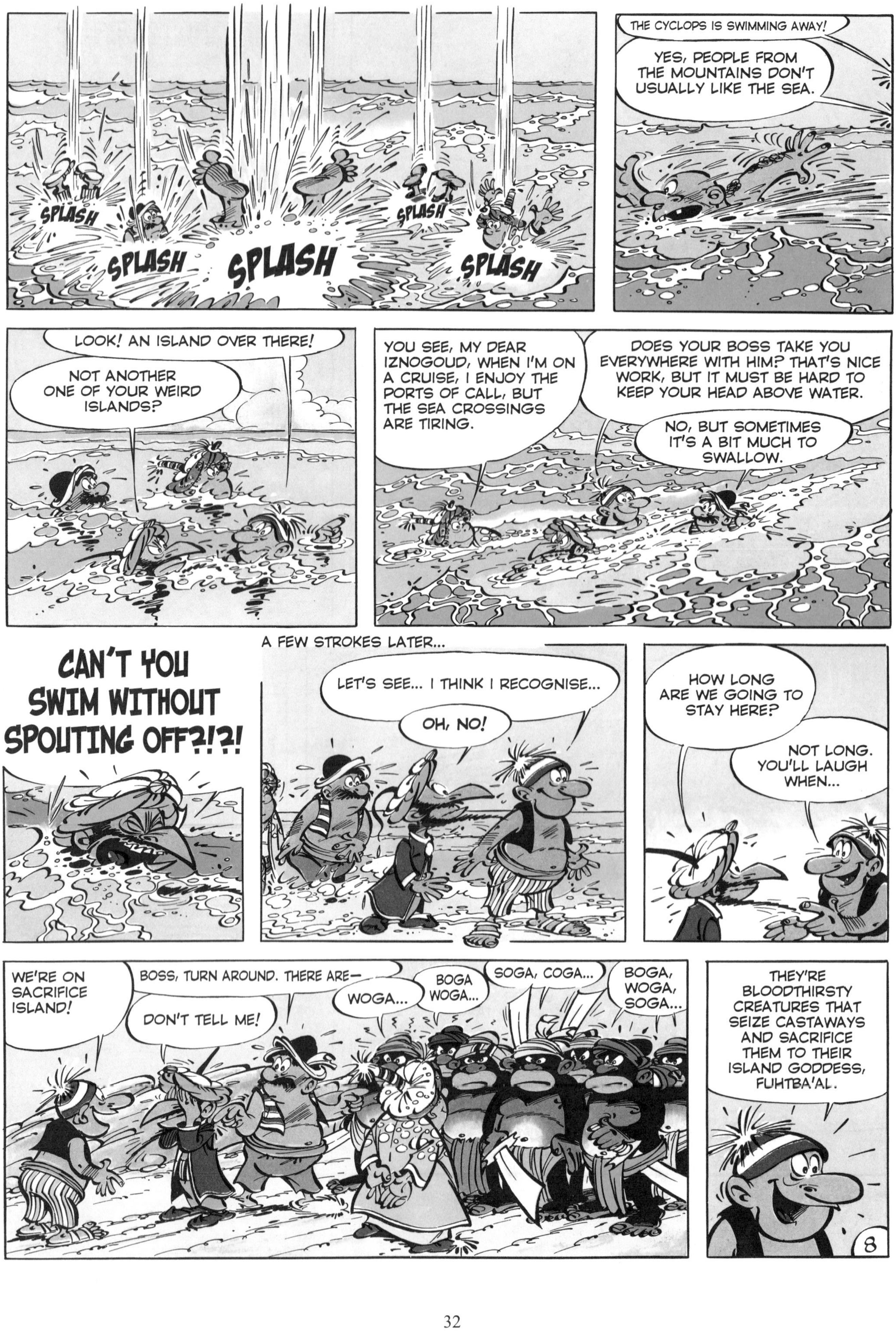
SPLASH
SPLASH
SPLASH
SPLASH
SPLASH
THE CYCLOPS IS SWIMMING AWAY!
YES, PEOPLE FROM THE MOUNTAINS DON'T USUALLY LIKE THE SEA.
LOOK! AN ISLAND OVER THERE!
NOT ANOTHER ONE OF YOUR WEIRD ISLANDS?
YOU SEE, MY DEAR IZNOGOUD, WHEN I'M ON A CRUISE, I ENJOY THE PORTS OF CALL, BUT THE SEA CROSSINGS ARE TIRING.
DOES YOUR BOSS TAKE YOU EVERYWHERE WITH HIM? THAT'S NICE WORK, BUT IT MUST BE HARD TO KEEP YOUR HEAD ABOVE WATER.
NO, BUT SOMETIMES IT'S A BIT MUCH TO SWALLOW.
CAN'T YOU SWIM WITHOUT SPOUTING OFF?!?!
A FEW STROKES LATER...
LET'S SEE... I THINK I RECOGNISE...
OH, NO!
HOW LONG ARE WE GOING TO STAY HERE?
NOT LONG. YOU'LL LAUGH WHEN...
WE'RE ON SACRIFICE ISLAND!
BOSS, TURN AROUND. THERE ARE—
DON'T TELL ME!
WOGA...
BOGA WOGA...
SOGA, COGA...
BOGA, WOGA, SOGA...
THEY'RE BLOODTHIRSTY CREATURES THAT SEIZE CASTAWAYS AND SACRIFICE THEM TO THEIR ISLAND GODDESS, FUHTBA'AL.
8

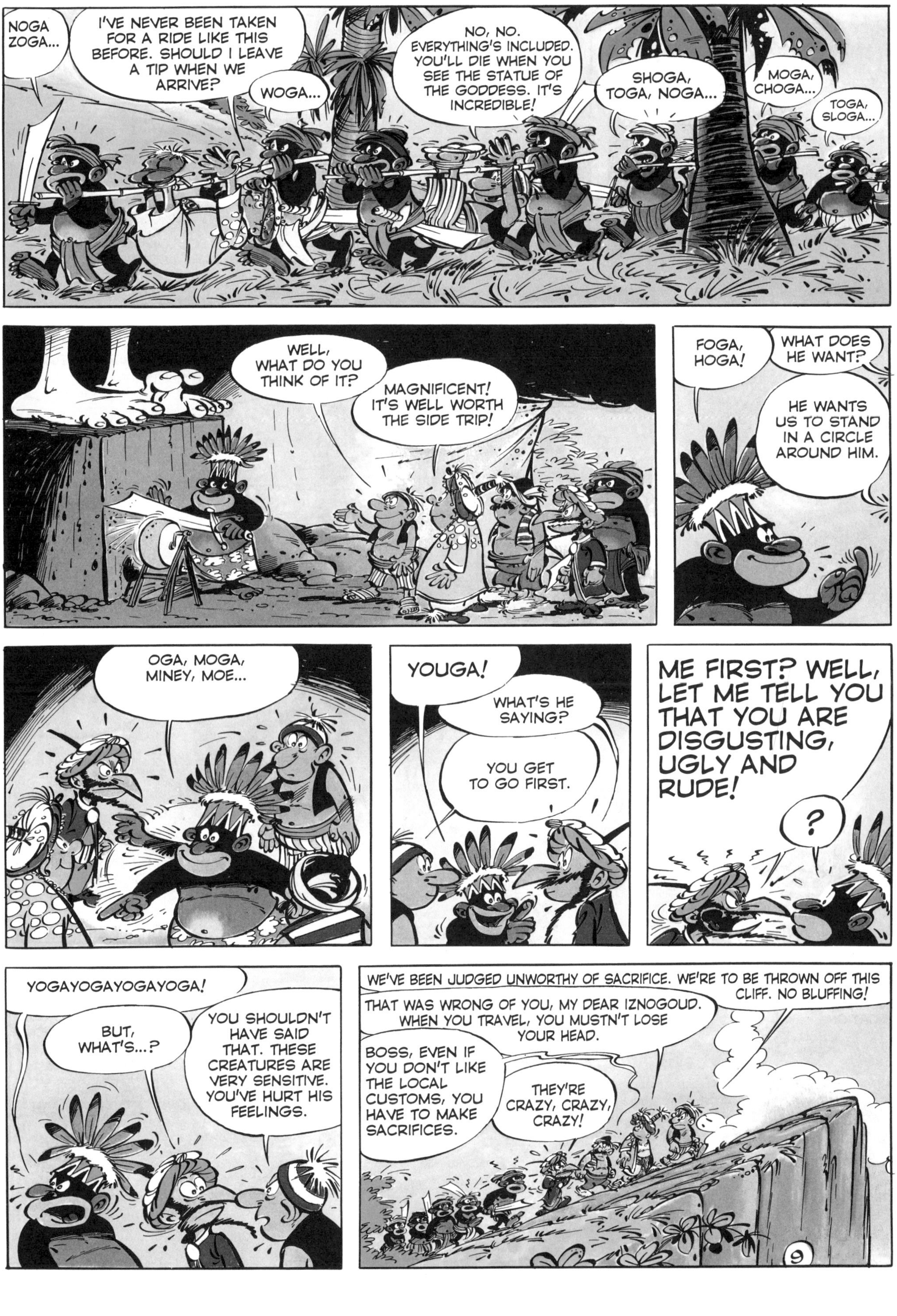

NOGA ZOGA...
I'VE NEVER BEEN TAKEN FOR A RIDE LIKE THIS BEFORE. SHOULD I LEAVE A TIP WHEN WE ARRIVE?
WOGA...
NO, NO. EVERYTHING'S INCLUDED. YOU'LL DIE WHEN YOU SEE THE STATUE OF THE GODDESS. IT'S INCREDIBLE!
SHOGA, TOGA, NOGA...
MOGA, CHOGA...
TOGA, SLOGA...
WELL, WHAT DO YOU THINK OF IT?
MAGNIFICENT! IT'S WELL WORTH THE SIDE TRIP!
FOGA, HOGA!
WHAT DOES HE WANT?
HE WANTS US TO STAND IN A CIRCLE AROUND HIM.
OGA, MOGA, MINEY, MOE...
YOUGA!
WHAT'S HE SAYING?
YOU GET TO GO FIRST.
ME FIRST? WELL, LET ME TELL YOU THAT YOU ARE DISGUSTING, UGLY AND RUDE!
?
YOGAYOGAYOGAYOGA!
BUT, WHAT'S...?
YOU SHOULDN'T HAVE SAID THAT. THESE CREATURES ARE VERY SENSITIVE. YOU'VE HURT HIS FEELINGS.
WE'VE BEEN JUDGED UNWORTHY OF SACRIFICE. WE'RE TO BE THROWN OFF THIS CLIFF. NO BLUFFING!
THAT WAS WRONG OF YOU, MY DEAR IZNOGOUD. WHEN YOU TRAVEL, YOU MUSTN'T LOSE YOUR HEAD.
BOSS, EVEN IF YOU DON'T LIKE THE LOCAL CUSTOMS, YOU HAVE TO MAKE SACRIFICES.
THEY'RE CRAZY, CRAZY, CRAZY!
9

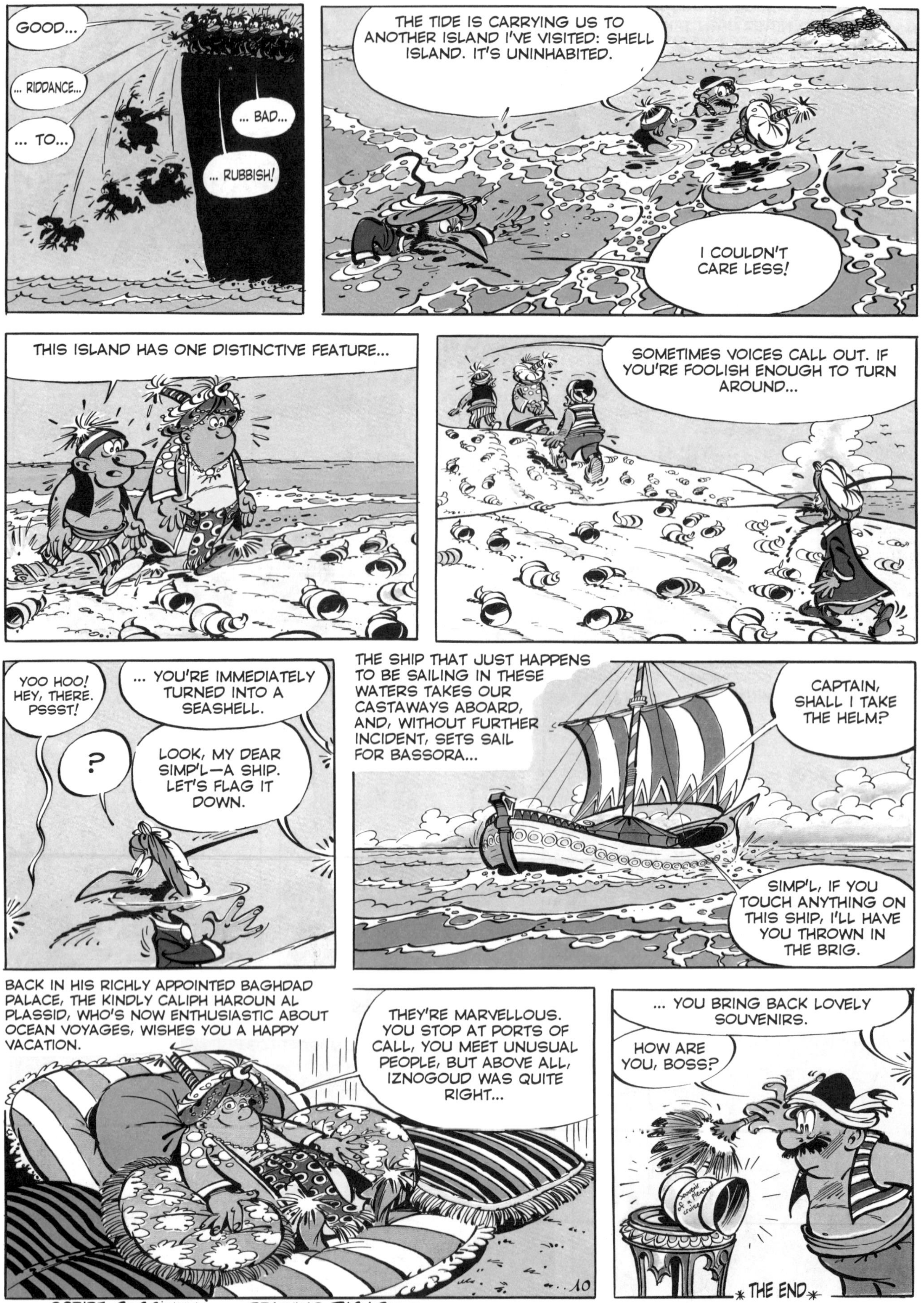
GOOD...
... RIDDANCE...
... TO...
... BAD...
... RUBBISH!
THE TIDE IS CARRYING US TO ANOTHER ISLAND I'VE VISITED: SHELL ISLAND. IT'S UNINHABITED.
I COULDN'T CARE LESS!
THIS ISLAND HAS ONE DISTINCTIVE FEATURE...
SOMETIMES VOICES CALL OUT. IF YOU'RE FOOLISH ENOUGH TO TURN AROUND...
YOO HOO! HEY, THERE. PSSST!
... YOU'RE IMMEDIATELY TURNED INTO A SEASHELL.
?
LOOK, MY DEAR SIMP'L—A SHIP. LET'S FLAG IT DOWN.
THE SHIP THAT JUST HAPPENS TO BE SAILING IN THESE WATERS TAKES OUR CASTAWAYS ABOARD, AND, WITHOUT FURTHER INCIDENT, SETS SAIL FOR BASSORA...
CAPTAIN, SHALL I TAKE THE HELM?
SIMP'L, IF YOU TOUCH ANYTHING ON THIS SHIP, I'LL HAVE YOU THROWN IN THE BRIG.
BACK IN HIS RICHLY APPOINTED BAGHDAD PALACE, THE KINDLY CALIPH HAROUN AL PLASSID, WHO'S NOW ENTHUSIASTIC ABOUT OCEAN VOYAGES, WISHES YOU A HAPPY VACATION.
THEY'RE MARVELLOUS. YOU STOP AT PORTS OF CALL, YOU MEET UNUSUAL PEOPLE, BUT ABOVE ALL, IZNOGOUD WAS QUITE RIGHT...
10
... YOU BRING BACK LOVELY SOUVENIRS.
HOW ARE YOU, BOSS?
* THE END *
SCRIPT: GOSCINNY - DRAWING: TABARY-62

LIHKWID'S BOTTLE OR THE BOTTLE OF LIHKWID

SCRIP: GOSCINNY
DRAWING: TABARY-66

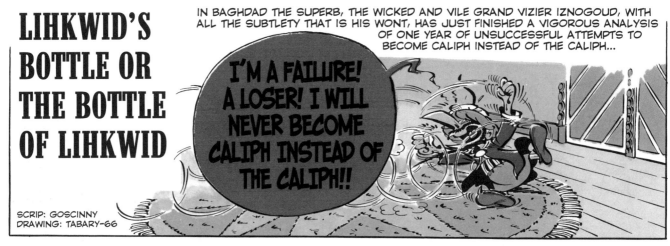

IN BAGHDAD THE SUPERB, THE WICKED AND VILE GRAND VIZIER IZNOGOUD, WITH ALL THE SUBTLETY THAT IS HIS WONT, HAS JUST FINISHED A VIGOROUS ANALYSIS OF ONE YEAR OF UNSUCCESSFUL ATTEMPTS TO BECOME CALIPH INSTEAD OF THE CALIPH...

I'M A FAILURE! A LOSER! I WILL NEVER BECOME CALIPH INSTEAD OF THE CALIPH!!

... WHEN FATE INTERVENES IN THE GUISE OF A...

... PEDDLER WHO'D LIKE TO SEE YOU, BOSS.

MY NAME IS LIHKWID, O GRAND VIZIER, AND I'VE GOT EVERYTHING YOU COULD EVER NEED.

I'D BE SURPRISED.

I'VE BROUGHT A LOT OF MERCHANDISE FROM FARAWAY PLACES. COME ON— I LEFT IT IN THE HALLWAY.

WHY NOT? I NEED SOMETHING TO DISTRACT ME FROM MY TROUBLES.

THERE. YOU SEE?

YOU DO OFFER A WIDE VARIETY, BUT I WONDER IF YOU HAVE WHAT I WANT...

JUST SAY THE WORD AND IT'S YOURS.

SOMETHING TO MAKE A CALIPH DISAPPEAR!

THAT'S EASY. I HAVE A SPECIAL BOTTLE—A RADICAL REMEDY FOR CALIPHS... EVEN RADICALIPHS... HEE HEE HEE!

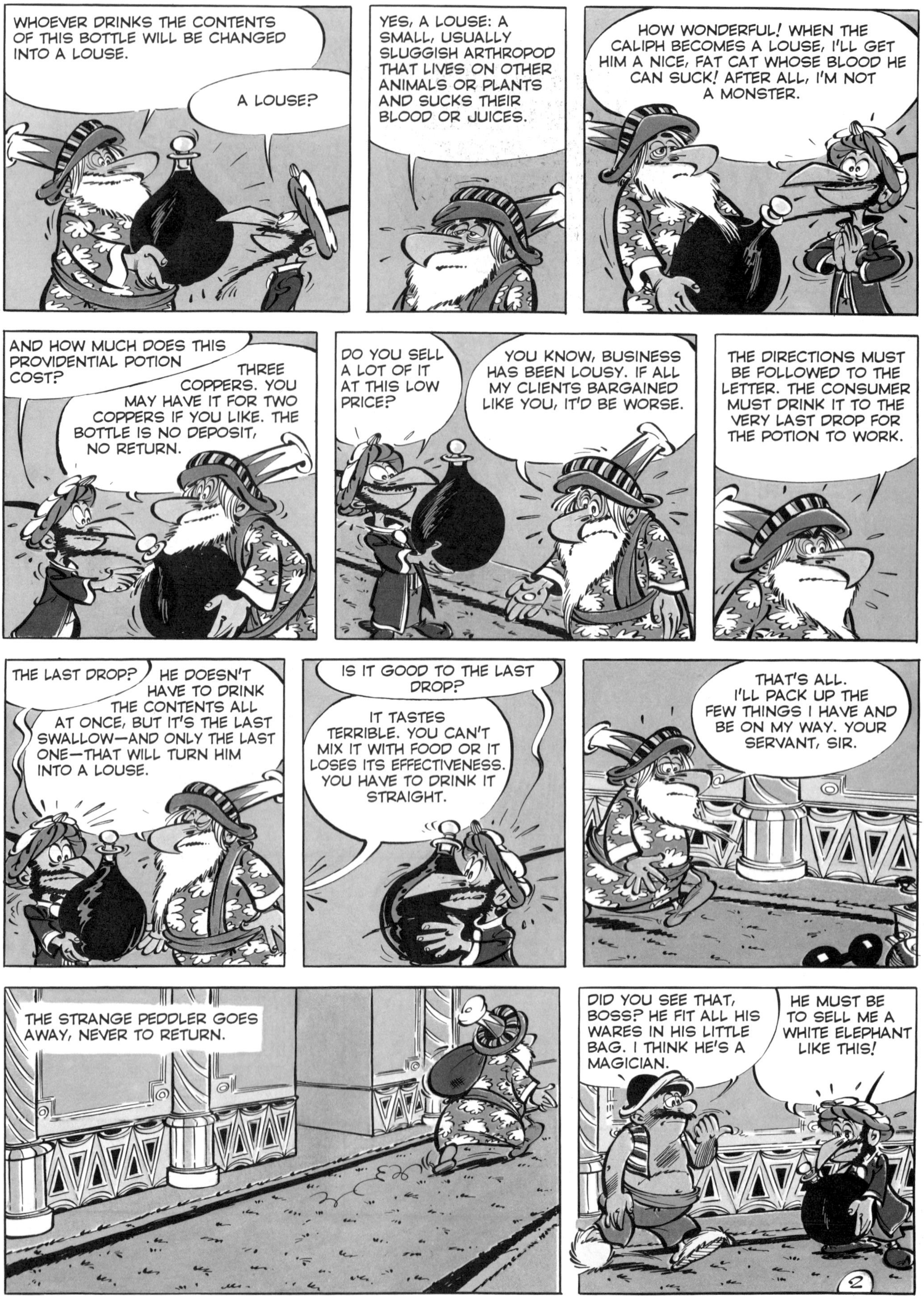
WHOEVER DRINKS THE CONTENTS OF THIS BOTTLE WILL BE CHANGED INTO A LOUSE.
A LOUSE?
YES, A LOUSE: A SMALL, USUALLY SLUGGISH ARTHROPOD THAT LIVES ON OTHER ANIMALS OR PLANTS AND SUCKS THEIR BLOOD OR JUICES.
HOW WONDERFUL! WHEN THE CALIPH BECOMES A LOUSE, I'LL GET HIM A NICE, FAT CAT WHOSE BLOOD HE CAN SUCK! AFTER ALL, I'M NOT A MONSTER.
AND HOW MUCH DOES THIS PROVIDENTIAL POTION COST?
THREE COPPERS. YOU MAY HAVE IT FOR TWO COPPERS IF YOU LIKE. THE BOTTLE IS NO DEPOSIT, NO RETURN.
DO YOU SELL A LOT OF IT AT THIS LOW PRICE?
YOU KNOW, BUSINESS HAS BEEN LOUSY. IF ALL MY CLIENTS BARGAINED LIKE YOU, IT'D BE WORSE.
THE DIRECTIONS MUST BE FOLLOWED TO THE LETTER. THE CONSUMER MUST DRINK IT TO THE VERY LAST DROP FOR THE POTION TO WORK.
THE LAST DROP?
HE DOESN'T HAVE TO DRINK THE CONTENTS ALL AT ONCE, BUT IT'S THE LAST SWALLOW—AND ONLY THE LAST ONE—THAT WILL TURN HIM INTO A LOUSE.
IS IT GOOD TO THE LAST DROP?
IT TASTES TERRIBLE. YOU CAN'T MIX IT WITH FOOD OR IT LOSES ITS EFFECTIVENESS. YOU HAVE TO DRINK IT STRAIGHT.
THAT'S ALL. I'LL PACK UP THE FEW THINGS I HAVE AND BE ON MY WAY. YOUR SERVANT, SIR.
THE STRANGE PEDDLER GOES AWAY, NEVER TO RETURN.
DID YOU SEE THAT, BOSS? HE FIT ALL HIS WARES IN HIS LITTLE BAG. I THINK HE'S A MAGICIAN.
HE MUST BE TO SELL ME A WHITE ELEPHANT LIKE THIS!

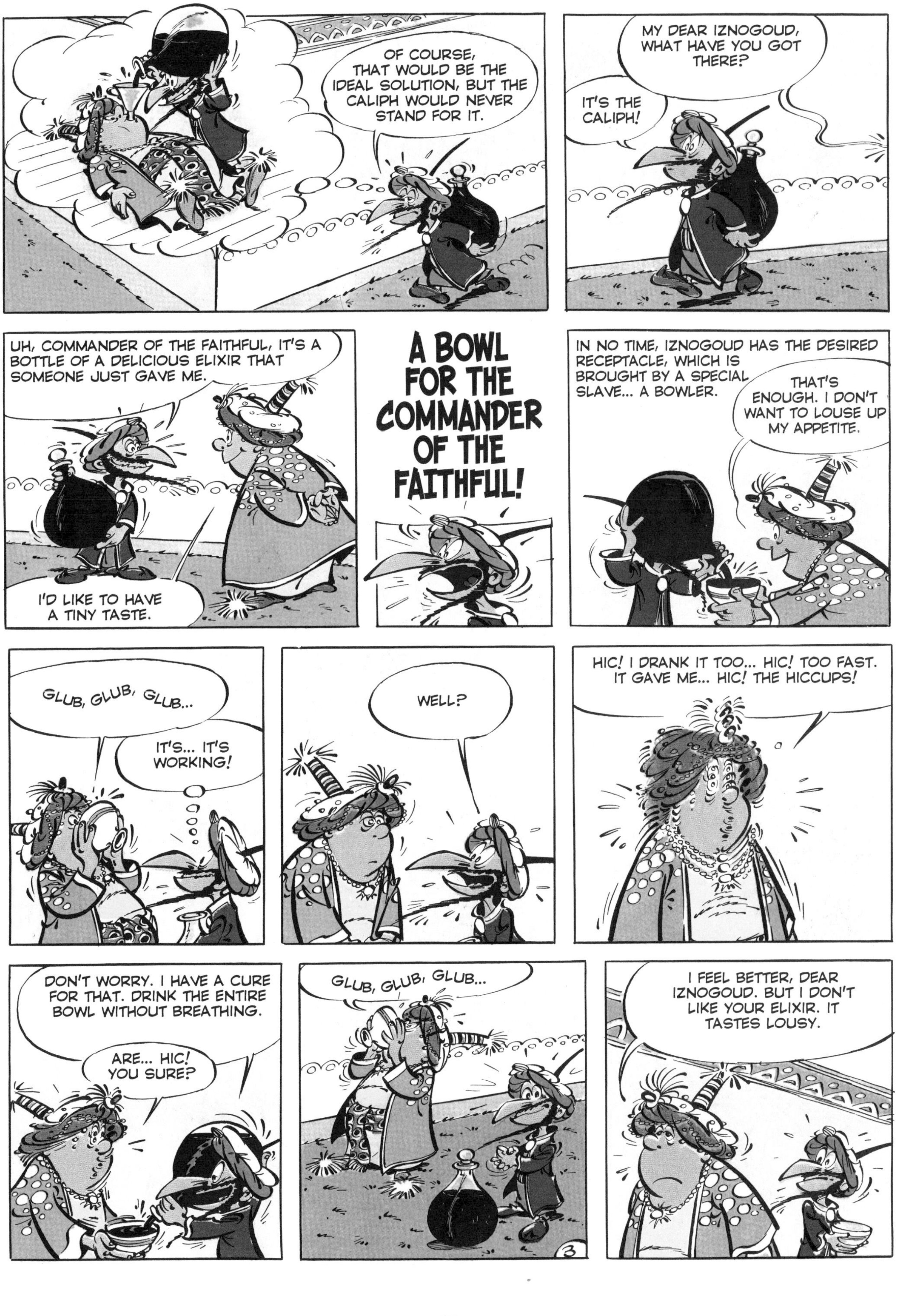

OF COURSE, THAT WOULD BE THE IDEAL SOLUTION, BUT THE CALIPH WOULD NEVER STAND FOR IT.
IT'S THE CALIPH!
MY DEAR IZNOGOUD, WHAT HAVE YOU GOT THERE?
UH, COMMANDER OF THE FAITHFUL, IT'S A BOTTLE OF A DELICIOUS ELIXIR THAT SOMEONE JUST GAVE ME.
I'D LIKE TO HAVE A TINY TASTE.
A BOWL FOR THE COMMANDER OF THE FAITHFUL!
IN NO TIME, IZNOGOUD HAS THE DESIRED RECEPTACLE, WHICH IS BROUGHT BY A SPECIAL SLAVE... A BOWLER.
THAT'S ENOUGH. I DON'T WANT TO LOUSE UP MY APPETITE.
GLUB, GLUB, GLUB...
IT'S... IT'S WORKING!
WELL?
HIC! I DRANK IT TOO... HIC! TOO FAST. IT GAVE ME... HIC! THE HICCUPS!
DON'T WORRY. I HAVE A CURE FOR THAT. DRINK THE ENTIRE BOWL WITHOUT BREATHING.
ARE... HIC! YOU SURE?
GLUB, GLUB, GLUB...
I FEEL BETTER, DEAR IZNOGOUD. BUT I DON'T LIKE YOUR ELIXIR. IT TASTES LOUSY.

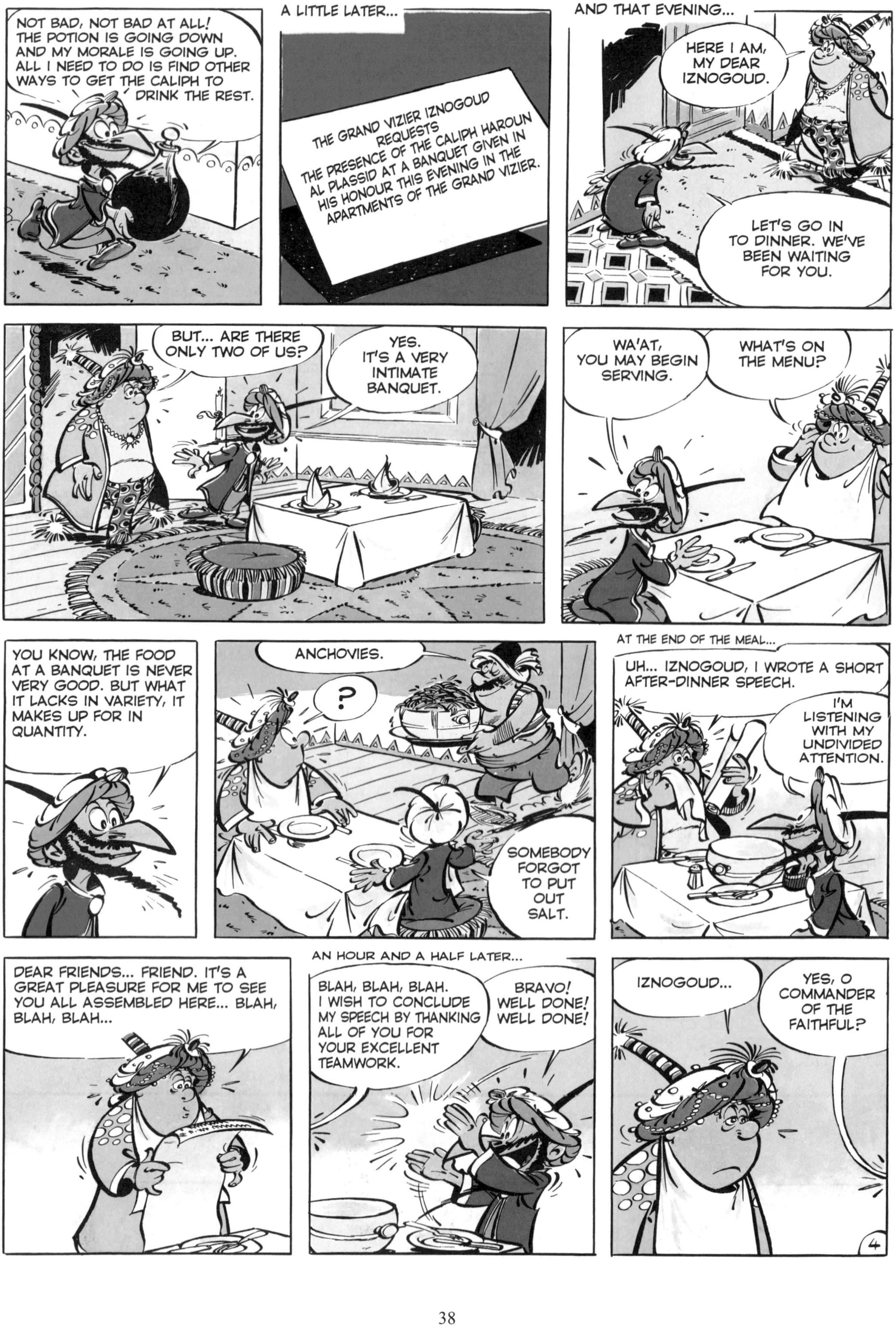
NOT BAD, NOT BAD AT ALL! THE POTION IS GOING DOWN AND MY MORALE IS GOING UP. ALL I NEED TO DO IS FIND OTHER WAYS TO GET THE CALIPH TO DRINK THE REST.
A LITTLE LATER...
THE GRAND VIZIER IZNOGOUD REQUESTS THE PRESENCE OF THE CALIPH HAROUN AL PLASSID AT A BANQUET GIVEN IN HIS HONOUR THIS EVENING IN THE APARTMENTS OF THE GRAND VIZIER.
AND THAT EVENING...
HERE I AM, MY DEAR IZNOGOUD.
LET'S GO IN TO DINNER. WE'VE BEEN WAITING FOR YOU.
BUT... ARE THERE ONLY TWO OF US?
YES. IT'S A VERY INTIMATE BANQUET.
WA'AT, YOU MAY BEGIN SERVING.
WHAT'S ON THE MENU?
YOU KNOW, THE FOOD AT A BANQUET IS NEVER VERY GOOD. BUT WHAT IT LACKS IN VARIETY, IT MAKES UP FOR IN QUANTITY.
ANCHOVIES.
?
SOMEBODY FORGOT TO PUT OUT SALT.
AT THE END OF THE MEAL...
UH... IZNOGOUD, I WROTE A SHORT AFTER-DINNER SPEECH.
I'M LISTENING WITH MY UNDIVIDED ATTENTION.
DEAR FRIENDS... FRIEND. IT'S A GREAT PLEASURE FOR ME TO SEE YOU ALL ASSEMBLED HERE... BLAH, BLAH, BLAH...
AN HOUR AND A HALF LATER...
BLAH, BLAH, BLAH. I WISH TO CONCLUDE MY SPEECH BY THANKING ALL OF YOU FOR YOUR EXCELLENT TEAMWORK.
BRAVO! WELL DONE! WELL DONE!
IZNOGOUD...
YES, O COMMANDER OF THE FAITHFUL?
4

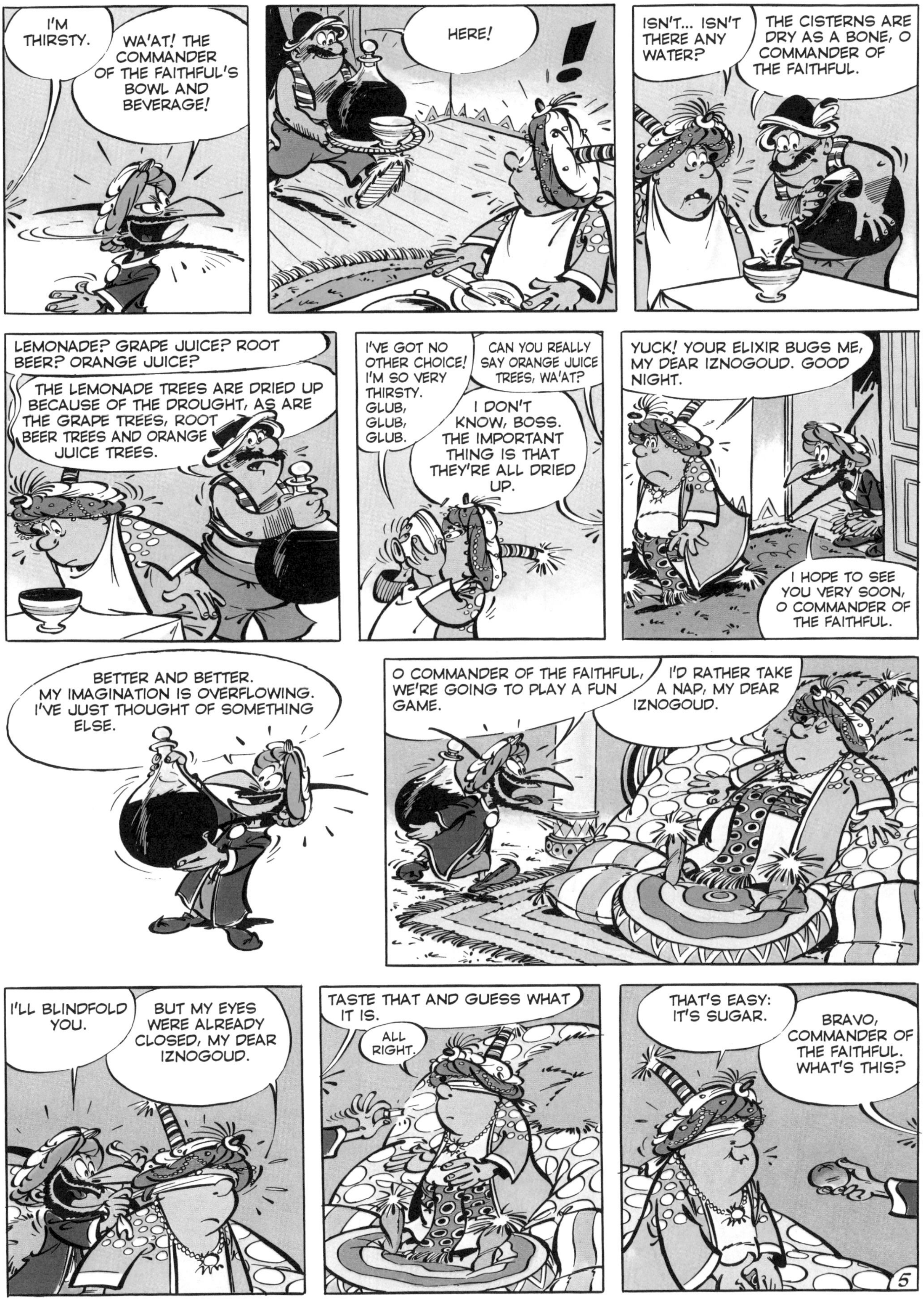
I'M THIRSTY.
WA'AT! THE COMMANDER OF THE FAITHFUL'S BOWL AND BEVERAGE!
HERE!
!
ISN'T... ISN'T THERE ANY WATER?
THE CISTERNS ARE DRY AS A BONE, O COMMANDER OF THE FAITHFUL.
LEMONADE? GRAPE JUICE? ROOT BEER? ORANGE JUICE?
THE LEMONADE TREES ARE DRIED UP BECAUSE OF THE DROUGHT, AS ARE THE GRAPE TREES, ROOT BEER TREES AND ORANGE JUICE TREES.
I'VE GOT NO OTHER CHOICE! I'M SO VERY THIRSTY. GLUB, GLUB, GLUB.
CAN YOU REALLY SAY ORANGE JUICE TREES, WA'AT?
I DON'T KNOW, BOSS. THE IMPORTANT THING IS THAT THEY'RE ALL DRIED UP.
YUCK! YOUR ELIXIR BUGS ME, MY DEAR IZNOGOUD. GOOD NIGHT.
I HOPE TO SEE YOU VERY SOON, O COMMANDER OF THE FAITHFUL.
BETTER AND BETTER. MY IMAGINATION IS OVERFLOWING. I'VE JUST THOUGHT OF SOMETHING ELSE.
O COMMANDER OF THE FAITHFUL, WE'RE GOING TO PLAY A FUN GAME.
I'D RATHER TAKE A NAP, MY DEAR IZNOGOUD.
I'LL BLINDFOLD YOU.
BUT MY EYES WERE ALREADY CLOSED, MY DEAR IZNOGOUD.
TASTE THAT AND GUESS WHAT IT IS.
ALL RIGHT.
THAT'S EASY: IT'S SUGAR.
BRAVO, COMMANDER OF THE FAITHFUL. WHAT'S THIS?
5

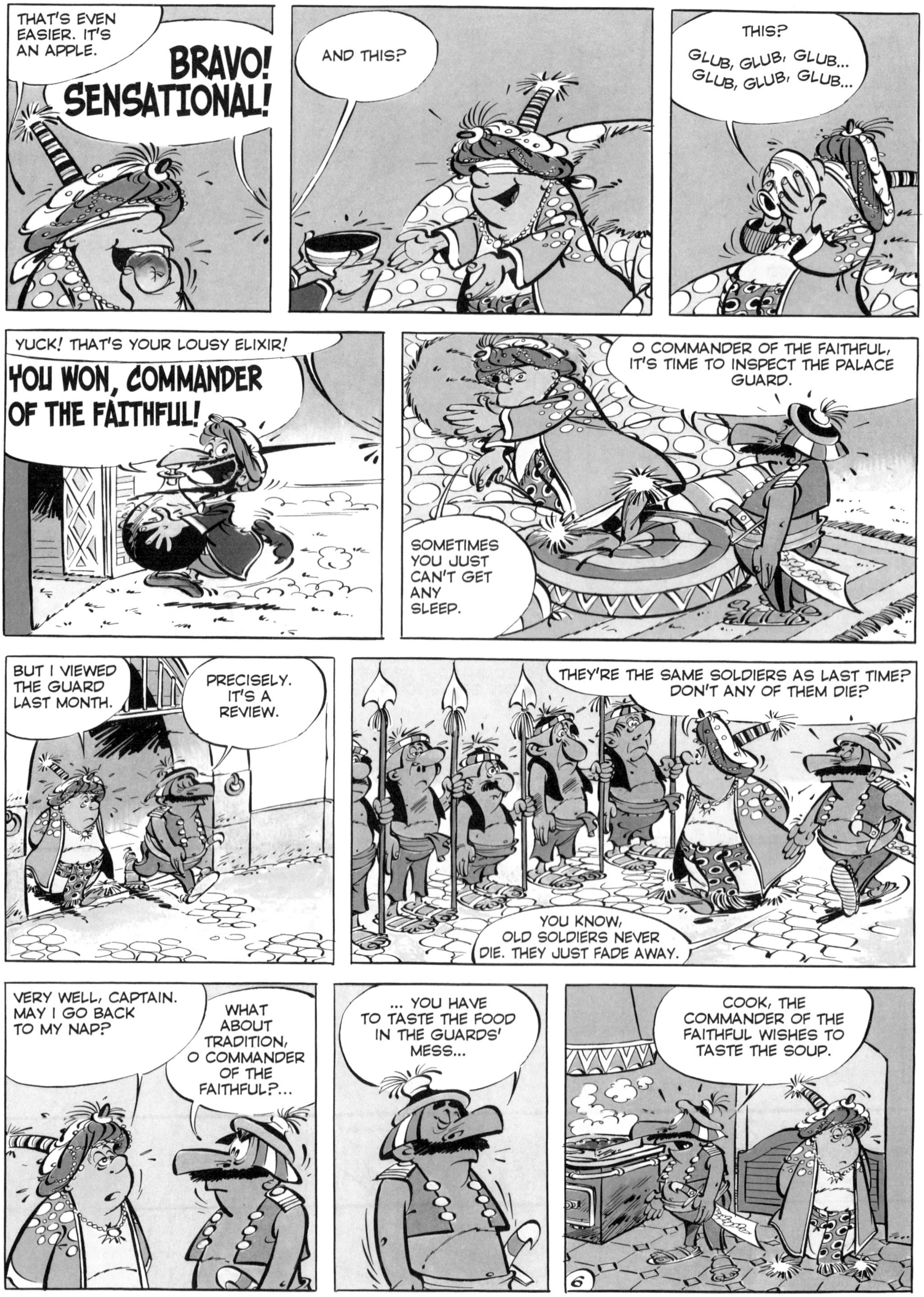
THAT'S EVEN EASIER. IT'S AN APPLE.
BRAVO! SENSATIONAL!
AND THIS?
THIS?
GLUB, GLUB, GLUB... GLUB, GLUB, GLUB...
YUCK! THAT'S YOUR LOUSY ELIXIR!
YOU WON, COMMANDER OF THE FAITHFUL!
O COMMANDER OF THE FAITHFUL, IT'S TIME TO INSPECT THE PALACE GUARD.
SOMETIMES YOU JUST CAN'T GET ANY SLEEP.
BUT I VIEWED THE GUARD LAST MONTH.
PRECISELY. IT'S A REVIEW.
THEY'RE THE SAME SOLDIERS AS LAST TIME? DON'T ANY OF THEM DIE?
YOU KNOW, OLD SOLDIERS NEVER DIE. THEY JUST FADE AWAY.
VERY WELL, CAPTAIN. MAY I GO BACK TO MY NAP?
WHAT ABOUT TRADITION, O COMMANDER OF THE FAITHFUL?...
... YOU HAVE TO TASTE THE FOOD IN THE GUARDS' MESS...
COOK, THE COMMANDER OF THE FAITHFUL WISHES TO TASTE THE SOUP.
6

GLUB, GLUB, GLUB...
GLUB, GLUB, GLUB...

WELL, COMMANDER OF THE FAITHFUL? IS IT GOOD?

NO. IT TASTES LIKE THAT TERRIBLE ELIXIR!

HEH, HEH, HEH!

THAT'S FUNNY. I FEEL A LITTLE BLOATED.

YOO HOO! COMMANDER OF THE FAITHFUL. I'VE GOT GOOD NEWS FOR YOU.

WHAT GOOD NEWS?

YOU HAVE BEEN CHOSEN FOR A GREAT HONOUR!

I'VE ALREADY BEEN AWARDED ALL OF THE GREAT HONOURS. I'M BLUE RIBBON OF THE HOLY COW, KNIGHT OF THE SQUARE TABLE...

SILVER TURBAN OF THE MARINATED ELEPHANT, DEFENDER OF THE MEEK OF HEART...

THIS IS EVEN MORE IMPRESSIVE. YOU'RE GOING TO BE INITIATED INTO A VERY EXCLUSIVE SOCIETY.

A VERY EXCLUSIVE SOCIETY?

WAIT FOR ME HERE. THE CEREMONY IS ABOUT TO BEGIN.

IT DOES SEEM IMPORTANT.

ENTER, INITIATE!

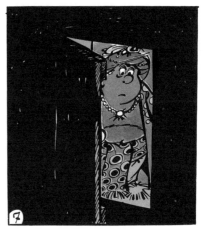

41

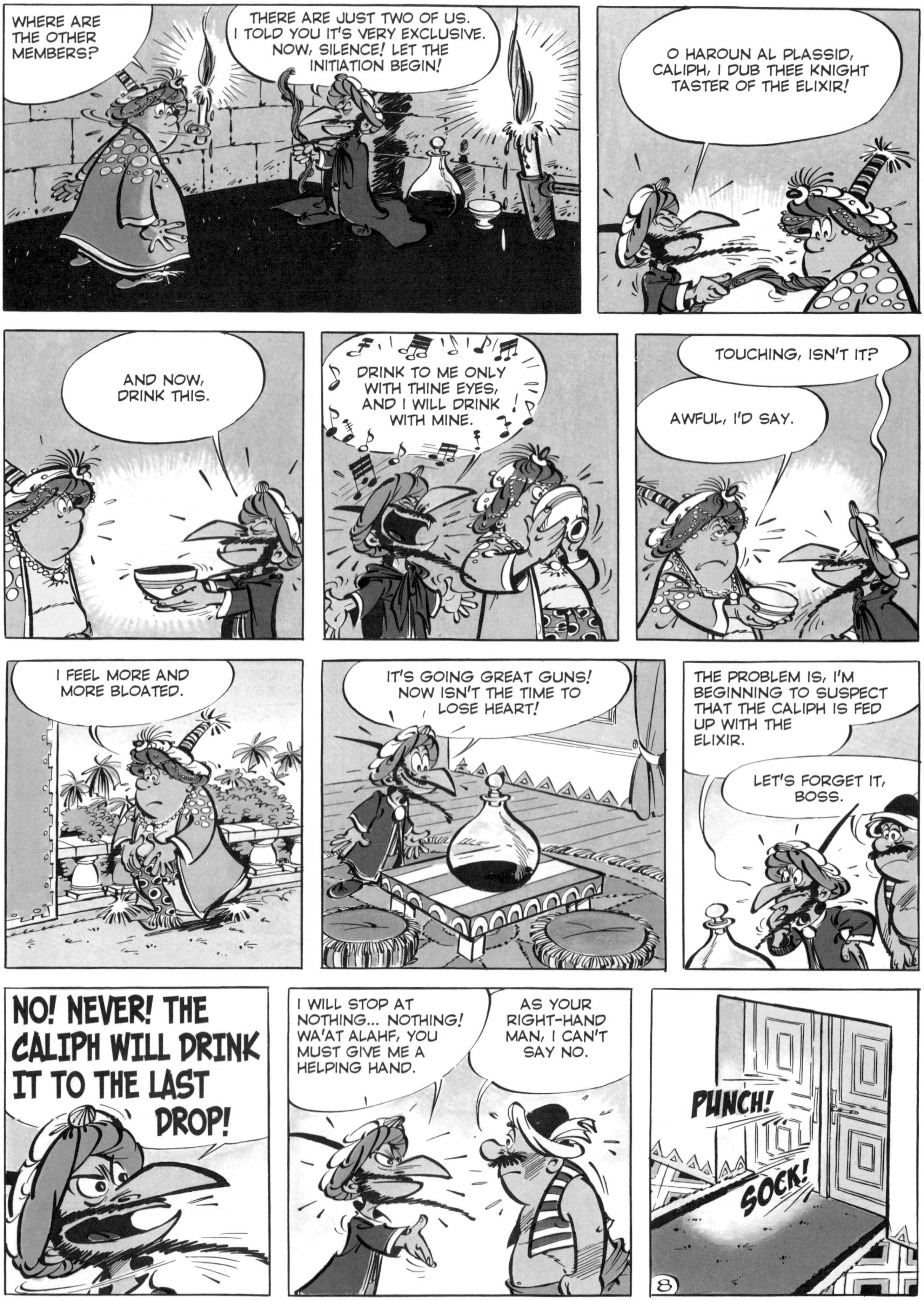
WHERE ARE THE OTHER MEMBERS?
THERE ARE JUST TWO OF US. I TOLD YOU IT'S VERY EXCLUSIVE. NOW, SILENCE! LET THE INITIATION BEGIN!
O HAROUN AL PLASSID, CALIPH, I DUB THEE KNIGHT TASTER OF THE ELIXIR!
AND NOW, DRINK THIS.
DRINK TO ME ONLY WITH THINE EYES, AND I WILL DRINK WITH MINE.
TOUCHING, ISN'T IT?
AWFUL, I'D SAY.
I FEEL MORE AND MORE BLOATED.
IT'S GOING GREAT GUNS! NOW ISN'T THE TIME TO LOSE HEART!
THE PROBLEM IS, I'M BEGINNING TO SUSPECT THAT THE CALIPH IS FED UP WITH THE ELIXIR.
LET'S FORGET IT, BOSS.
NO! NEVER! THE CALIPH WILL DRINK IT TO THE LAST DROP!
I WILL STOP AT NOTHING... NOTHING! WA'AT ALAHF, YOU MUST GIVE ME A HELPING HAND.
AS YOUR RIGHT-HAND MAN, I CAN'T SAY NO.
PUNCH!
SOCK!
8

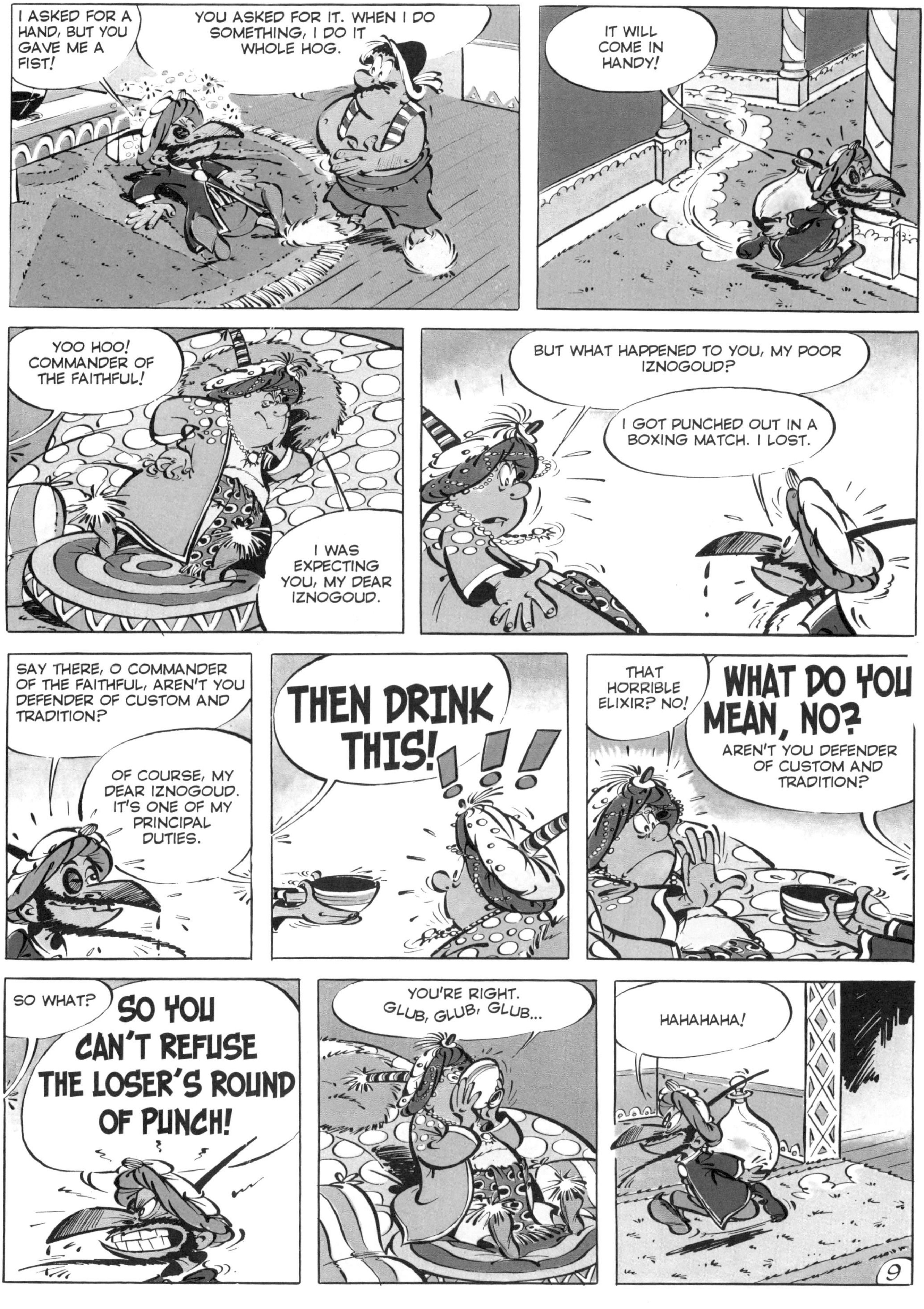
I ASKED FOR A HAND, BUT YOU GAVE ME A FIST!
YOU ASKED FOR IT. WHEN I DO SOMETHING, I DO IT WHOLE HOG.
IT WILL COME IN HANDY!
YOO HOO! COMMANDER OF THE FAITHFUL!
I WAS EXPECTING YOU, MY DEAR IZNOGOUD.
BUT WHAT HAPPENED TO YOU, MY POOR IZNOGOUD?
I GOT PUNCHED OUT IN A BOXING MATCH. I LOST.
SAY THERE, O COMMANDER OF THE FAITHFUL, AREN'T YOU DEFENDER OF CUSTOM AND TRADITION?
OF COURSE, MY DEAR IZNOGOUD. IT'S ONE OF MY PRINCIPAL DUTIES.
THEN DRINK THIS!
!!!
THAT HORRIBLE ELIXIR? NO!
WHAT DO YOU MEAN, NO?
AREN'T YOU DEFENDER OF CUSTOM AND TRADITION?
SO WHAT?
SO YOU CAN'T REFUSE THE LOSER'S ROUND OF PUNCH!
YOU'RE RIGHT. GLUB, GLUB, GLUB...
HAHAHAHA!
9

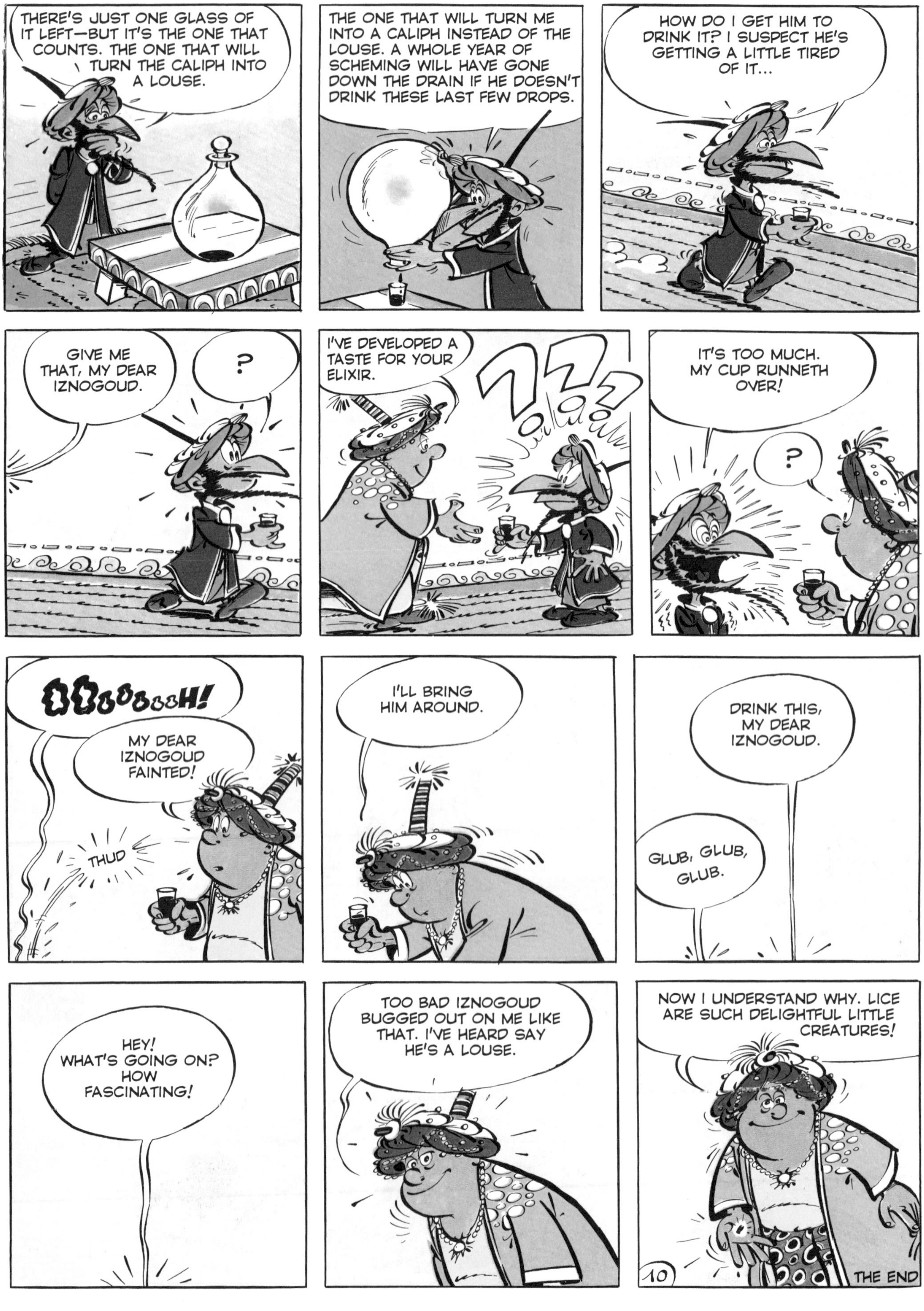
THERE'S JUST ONE GLASS OF IT LEFT—BUT IT'S THE ONE THAT COUNTS. THE ONE THAT WILL TURN THE CALIPH INTO A LOUSE.
THE ONE THAT WILL TURN ME INTO A CALIPH INSTEAD OF THE LOUSE. A WHOLE YEAR OF SCHEMING WILL HAVE GONE DOWN THE DRAIN IF HE DOESN'T DRINK THESE LAST FEW DROPS.
HOW DO I GET HIM TO DRINK IT? I SUSPECT HE'S GETTING A LITTLE TIRED OF IT...
GIVE ME THAT, MY DEAR IZNOGOUD.
?
I'VE DEVELOPED A TASTE FOR YOUR ELIXIR.
???
IT'S TOO MUCH. MY CUP RUNNETH OVER!
?
OOOooooH!
MY DEAR IZNOGOUD FAINTED!
THUD
I'LL BRING HIM AROUND.
DRINK THIS, MY DEAR IZNOGOUD.
GLUB, GLUB, GLUB.
HEY! WHAT'S GOING ON? HOW FASCINATING!
TOO BAD IZNOGOUD BUGGED OUT ON ME LIKE THAT. I'VE HEARD SAY HE'S A LOUSE.
NOW I UNDERSTAND WHY. LICE ARE SUCH DELIGHTFUL LITTLE CREATURES!
10
THE END

IZNOGOUD

1 - THE WICKED WILES OF IZNOGOUD

2 - THE CALIPH'S VACATION

COMING SOON

3 - IZNOGOUD
AND THE DAY OF MISRULE
MARCH 2009

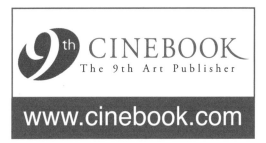

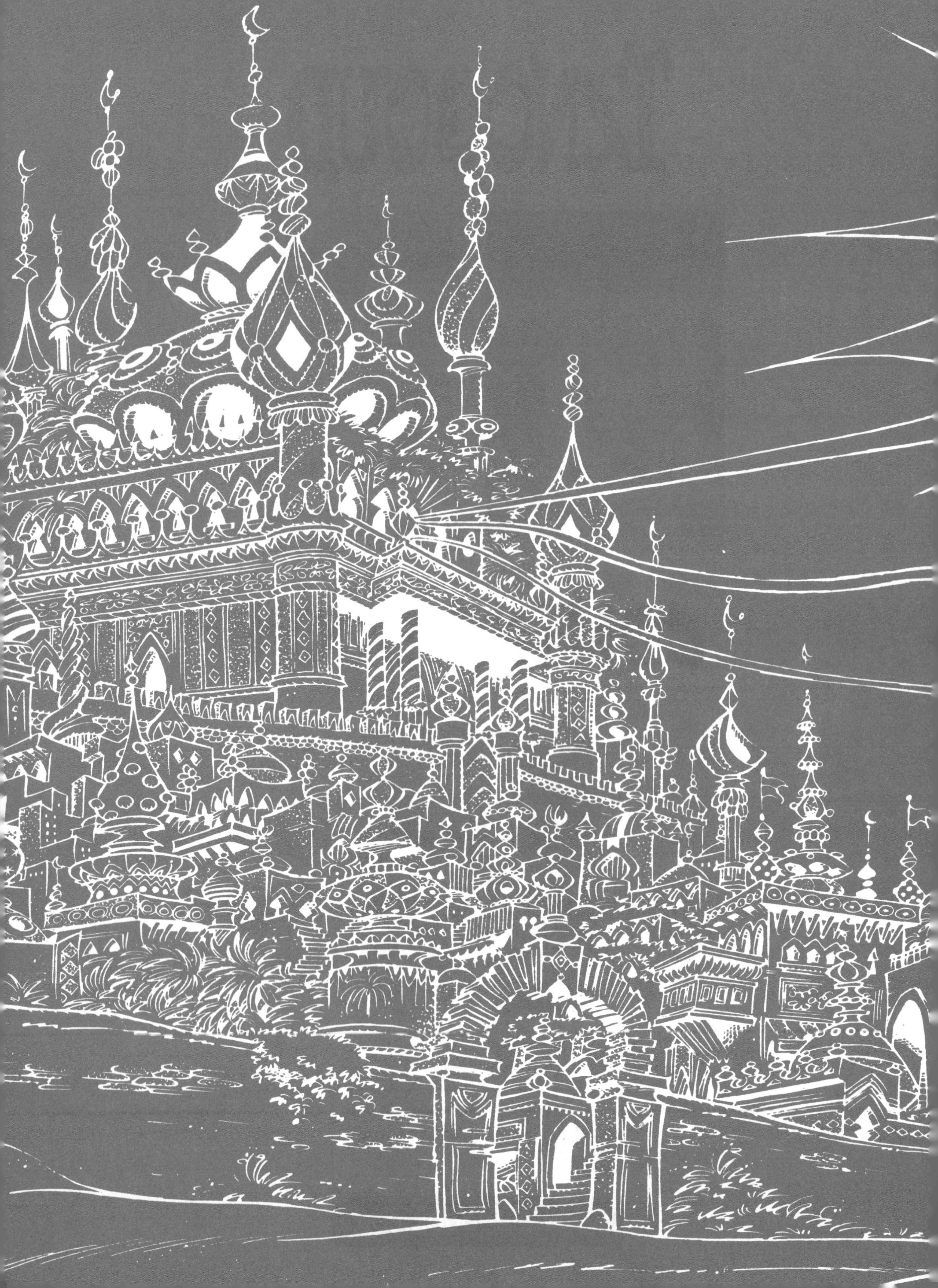